"A Constructed Murder"
Cozy Mystery

A Lone Peak Hotel Mystery
Volume Thirteen

Kendall Scott

This story is a work of fiction. Names, characters, businesses, places, events and incidents are the products of the author's imagination or used in a fictitious manner & are not to be construed as real. Any resemblance to actual persons, living or dead, or actual events is purely coincidental. Products or brand names mentioned are trademarks of their respective holders or companies. The cover uses licensed images & are shown for illustrative purposes only. Any person(s) that may be depicted on the cover are simply models.

Edition v1.00 (2021.09.28)

Special thanks to the volunteer readers who helped with proofreading. Thank you so much for your support.

Chapter One

Despite her best efforts, Constance just couldn't bring herself to settle on a single style of font for the title-page. And it wasn't so much that she didn't like any of the font choices either. It was more to do with the fact that none really seemed to capture the essence that was The Lone Peak Hotel.

"This one is a little glamorous," she noted of a style called 'Whizz Bang!' She highlighted the text, selected the font style and grimaced as the words on the page began to sparkle and shine. "And this one is a little... too much," she mused as she selected a style called 'Extravaganza!'

"You need to pick one." Jonas leaned over her shoulder and pointed toward a style that was simply labeled 'To the Point.' "This one is simple and easy."

"Too simple," Constance countered. She selected the style, highlighted the title page and changed the font. As she had expected, it was simple and boring, not worthy of The Lone Peak Hotel. "Far too simple."

"How about..." Jonas pondered as he eyed the different font types. His finger hovered over a few choices on the laptop screen, only for him to sense Constance's reservation at each one. "How about we move on from font styles for now? We can always come back to it later."

"That seems a little redundant," Constance protested.

"It's that or this website never gets finished.".

"And wouldn't that be a shame," Constance said bitterly. She hated that she was forced to do this. Hated it! But as Jonas had pointed out – and Eleanor, and Sydney, and everyone else she had spoken to – times were changing and The Lone Peak had to either adapt or fall behind. There was no way that Constance was going to fall behind.

"Fiiiiiiiine," she sighed as she exited from the font choices, circling back to the top of the page. "What's next? Let's get this done shall we, so I can get a start on never having to think about it again."

Constance Aberfield was a lot of things. She was sharp. She was quick. She was inquisitive. She was funny, clever, and friendly. She was caring, loving, and inviting. She was an avid reader, and a best-selling author. She was a good friend to those close to her, and a better wife to the man to whom she was married. Constance Aberfield was a lot of things, but she was not, by any stretch of the imagination, tech savvy.

Sitting down at her office desk, Constance was beginning to feel a little on edge. Her face was scrunched up tight and her brow narrowed to such a degree that her brows touched one another. Her face grew more and more red by the minute, and her right knee bobbed up and down relentlessly – a direct symptom of hours of suppressed irritation.

Standing behind her, leaning over her right shoulder, was her husband, Jonas. An absolute dish of a man; his dark features were framed by a square brow, a strong jaw, and just a hint of silver in his otherwise jet-black hair. A rather tall man too, he was forced to bend his knees and arch his back as he leaned forward and over Constance.

Also standing behind Constance, but leaning over her left shoulder, was The Lone Peak's most recent hire, Dakota (no last name was given). Twenty years old, but with a round baby-face that would put her closer to fifteen, Dakota had the look of a person that was never fully in the room. Her big, bright eyes wandered aimlessly as she spoke, giving the impression that she was always thinking about something else.

Dakota had been working for Constance and The Lone Peak for nearly three months now. Having walked in off the street one day looking for a job, it just so happened to be at the exact time that Eleanor, Constance's cleaning lady, was asking for more time off so she could go and visit her boyfriend who lived in L.A. Timing was everything, and Dakota took full advantage of that.

More to the point, where she was only supposed to be a casual hire, Sydney, The Lone Peak's receptionist, was soon asking for an entire month off so that she and her boyfriend could travel through South America. Again, Dakota just happened to be in the room and again she benefited mightily from it.

Three months now and Dakota had made herself all but indispensable at The Lone Peak Hotel. This was shocking to Constance, as the woman was absolutely hopeless when it came to just about everything.

In front of Constance, and the object of everyone's attention, was a newly purchased laptop. It had a name and a number too – like a darn spaceship or something – but darn if Constance knew what it was. Jonas told her it was the best, so she bought it. And it was as simple as that.

"I really like Extravaganza," Dakota mused to herself from over Constance's shoulder. "I like the sparkle." As usual, Dakota was about two conversations behind.

In front of the three was the open laptop, currently opened on The Lone Peak's first and only website. But from what Constance understood, the website wasn't live yet – whatever that meant? She was still editing and formatting the thing, bringing it up to a standard in line with the expectations of The Lone Peak Hotel. Heck, if this thing was going to be seen by everyone in the world then it had to be good!

"Oh!" Dakota suddenly grabbed onto Constance's shoulder. "Your handle. What is it? We can put it under contact info." She blinked her big, blue eyes at Constance and smiled an innocent, almost-goofy, smile.

"My what?"

"Your handle – twitter is probably best. That way, people can tweet when they stay here – oh! I can tweet while I work!" She beamed down at Constance, looking like a puppy waiting for praise.

"Tweet when they... what are you saying? Are those words – Jonas?! Do you have any idea what she's saying?" Constance leaned back and looked to her husband for support. He was the same age as she – sitting a little too north of fifty – but he was also 'in with the younger people,' as he claimed.

"Nothing you have to worry about," he chuckled and shook his head. Constance guessed that he didn't have a darn clue either and just didn't want to admit it.

"Will you speak English girl!" Constance snapped at Dakota. "Or German... but slowly. I'm a little rusty."

"I didn't know you spoke German!" Jonas exclaimed.

"There's a lot you don't know about me," she said with a wiry smirk. She was then back on Dakota. "Well?"

"Ahhhhh... do you have a phone number?" Dakota offered.

"What does that —"

"We can put that in contacts instead!" She pointed down at the screen, toward a section of the page that read 'contact.'

"And that's like a handle?" Constance asked. Even saying it sounded weird, and she was sure that she hadn't used it right.

"Sure!" Dakota exclaimed.

Somehow, Constance doubted it. But she chose to say nothing and let that very odd conversation die. With both Jonas and Dakota looking at her expectantly, she got about putting in all forms of contact for herself and the hotel – a single number and email address – all the while praying that this horrible experience was nearly over.

"Is that it?" she asked cautiously, sure that Jonas and Dakota would both shoot her down.

"I don't know...." Jonas leaned over Constance and took control of the laptop. "Let me just..."

As mentioned, Constance, Jonas, and Dakota were currently in the process of creating The Lone Peak Hotel's first ever website. All of it, from start to finish. When the idea was first pitched, Constance had assumed that they just bought a 'space,' wrote down some information about the hotel, and that was it. But oh no. That was too simple. That was too boring. That simply would not do.

Instead, they 'built' a page – at least that was what Jonas had said. It was a whole process of setting up rooms, taking photos, editing the photos, choosing layouts, writing descriptions... they even wanted her to upload the menu for the in-house restaurant. She tried to explain that the specials changed every day, so Jonas insisted that the base menu could still go up. She then tried to argue that it would be incomplete and he argued back... well, it went on for some time. The menu was now uploaded to the site.

It was a tremendous process and not one that Constance had at all expected, or enjoyed. The problem was that she just wasn't tech savvy, at all. She was all thumbs when it came to using anything even remotely electrical, and she was certain that this webpage would have only taken a normal person a few minutes... as opposed to two whole days!

The only reason that Constance had agreed to make a page in the first place was because she had no choice. As of the current moment, there was a huge highway-construction project happening not ten miles out of Modest Peak. It was part of a new superhighway intersecting through middle-America, shortening the trip by a huge amount by bypassing all the small country towns on the way. That included Modest Peak.

The little mountain town of Modest Peak, home to less than five thousand people, the kind of town where everyone knew one another, the kind of town where there was one of everything, and no need for anymore, the kind of town where even tourists felt like locals, was getting bypassed.

"I don't know how the store is going to survive!" It was over a month ago when news of the bypass first reached Modest Peak. Upon hearing the news,

Jonas had left work and sprinted right to The Lone Peak Hotel so he could inform Constance. "Let alone this place!"

Constance had been behind the reception counter at the time, thankfully in an empty room. The news had caught her off guard too, but for some reason she just wasn't as worried as Jonas had been. "It will be fine," she had assured him. "We'll manage."

"How?" Jonas has asked desperately. "I mean, the store will still putter along. Most of my business is local, anyhow. But this place lives by highway traffic. You know it does."

"I just know we will be," Constance had responded calmly. Again, she just wasn't that concerned.

Truth be told, the hotel was no longer at the top of Constance's priority list. She owned the hotel, and the land it was built upon. She had no rental obligation, or fears of it being repossessed. And ever since she had gotten married some six months previously, she'd found that the hotel featured less prominently in her future... or at least where she saw her future headed.

So, if the hotel did quiet down a little, so be it. Even if she had to close it during the quieter months, or only open it for holidays or something along those lines. The Lone Peak would live on, in some form or another. It was odd too that she was starting to think this way, as it was a train of thought that she never, ever would have believed possible. But being married to the man of her dreams was bound to have an effect on her.

Jonas, the man of her dreams, wasn't nearly as calm as she. He carried on, and on, and on about what would happen, until Dakota drifted into the room and interjected with, "Make sure you mention the bypass on the website too. So people don't get lost."

Jonas and Constance had both paused, turned and looked at Dakota, who remained standing idly in the middle of the room, eyes staring up at the ceiling. "Website?" Constance had said. "We don't have one." And that was how the idea for a website started.

With the bypass now in progress, making a website for the Lone Peak just seemed logical, and that was why Constance was making one. She had just never dreamed it would be so darn challenging. Whatever happened to the old days where you would take out a single page add in the local paper? Or hand out fliers or something like that. So much easier! And that wasn't to say that Constance was against the idea of change per se, she just wished that it would slow down... just a touch.

"... looks good!" Jonas finished up scrolling through the now finished website. "Shall we... go live?" he raised his eyebrows while smirking like an idiot.

"I'd rather you just go," she said back, under her breath but just loud enough so that he would hear. Then, "Sure – oh! The fonts!" She beat her hands on the table in frustration. "I completely forgot."

"Oh yeah..." Jonas grimaced.

"Oh! I like 'Fairy Princess!'" Dakota announced, leaning over Constance shoulder, taking control of the laptop and selecting the font types. "It makes the whole page come alive."

Constance was done. At least for the night. Her back hurt from sitting, her eyes hurt from reading, and her hand hurt from controlling the laptop. As said, she had long since admitted that this webpage was a necessary evil, but that didn't mean she had to enjoy doing it.

"I think it's time to call it a night..." Constance started.

"No you don't!" Jonas cut in, his hand resting on her shoulder.

"You need to finish!" Dakota agreed.

Constance body seized up as her eyes darted around the room, looking for a way out. What she needed was a distraction. Lucky for her, one came not a second later.

A tremendous crash suddenly sounded from the outside the room, coming from the foyer of the hotel. It sounded to her like a body falling into something brittle, only to be joined a second later by the sudden eruption of raucous laughter and cheering. All male voices, at least four of them.

Constance's blood went cold as she listened to the men laughing and carrying on. Her eyes narrowed as she imagined them, traipsing mud through her hotel, annoying the other guests without care or concern. "I'll be one moment," she said coldly as she pushed herself to her feet.

Jonas didn't try and stop her this time, nor did Dakota. The two took a step back, allowing Constance space to stand. And then, once she was standing, they didn't say so much as a word as she stepped around the desk and headed for the door, the foyer, the source of the disturbance.

The whole thing was slightly overdone, to be honest. And although Constance was angry, she wasn't as rueful as she had let it seem. But she knew that acting so would make it easier to leave un-accosted, and she had been looking for a way out of that room after all.

Chapter Two

The source of the disturbance was a group of hotel guests, arriving back after what was presumably a long day of work. And where ordinarily, Constance wouldn't get herself into a state over a little bit of noise... there was nothing ordinary, or little, about this particular occurrence.

The laughter and jeering and general mayhem was still in full swing as Constance stormed into the hotel's lobby. Even when the four men – three primary antagonists – responsible for the noise spotted Constance coming for them, they continued to laugh, shout and carry on like they weren't in a hotel filled with other guests.

"What is going – what happened?!" Constance asked aghast as she took in the scene for the first time. "My table!"

Of the four men in the room, three of them were standing, knee slapping and laughing so darn hard that they had to hold on to one another for support. The fourth man was sprawled along the ground, his body laying atop what was now a broken, destroyed, unfixable, coffee table. The man himself looked fine, if not a little broken and bruised. The table, though, would need to be thrown out.

"Had himself a little fall," a tall, lanky, and rather smelly man that Constance knew simply as Slim-Jim, cackled as he wiped tears from his eyes.

"Holidays don't start for another three months, but he wants to take a trip early!" A short, chubby, rotund character that Constance had heard called Piggly-Pete chortled as he held onto his large belly.

"He said that he heard the table insult his mother, so naturally he had no choice but to defend her honor!" The third man chuckled in delight. His name was Tex-Mex, a cowboy-type with overly-tanned, cracked skin, a permanent five o'clock shadow on his square jaw, and a slow drawl in everything he said.

"I fell, is all!" The fourth man groaned. He was still laying on the floor, but had since managed to roll himself over and onto his back. His name was Stu; a dorky character with glasses, a comb over, an overbite and ears that seemed to stick straight out from his head. "I didn't mean it... I'm sorry, Ms. Aberfield."

"Sorry?! What on Earth for!" Slim-Jim cackled. "We paying for it!"

"Yeah!" Piggly-Pete agreed, nodding his head furiously, his five chins wobbling up and down as he did. "We should be able to break anything we like."

"Now, now," Tex-Mex eased. He stepped forward and offered a hand to Stu, still laying on the ground. "This 'ere is her establishment. She has the right to be a little touched." He held his hand out for Stu on the ground to take. Stu, seeing the hand, smiled gratefully, took the hand, was lifted a few inches off the ground when Tex-Mex suddenly let go.

Stu was caught completely off guard by the sudden reversal, and as a result, fell straight back to the ground with another crash. This sent the three men into a fresh state of hysterics; they fell over one another, cackling, laughing, cheering to themselves. It was quite the ruckus.

Constance was seething. She was boiling. She could feel the steam literally pouring from her ears and nose as she struggled to contain her anger. She had dealt with some problem guests in her time, but never, ever, ever had she had to put up with the likes of this lot. In years to come, when Constance was old and retired, she was sure that she'd look back on this particular group of people and remember them as the worst ever.

"I have other guests," Constance hissed. "And I would appreciate it if —"

"We're just going now," Tex-Mex cut her off. "No need to get your panties all twisted, ma'am." His smirk was repulsive, made worse by the wink he offered when he finished speaking.

"You'd think we were stayin' 'ere free of charge!" Slim-Jim complained.

"Yeah!" Piggly-Pete joined in.

The three men converged on one another, nodding their agreement that Constance was being unhelpful and a little tightly wound. Meanwhile, Stu was forced to push himself back up to his feet and dust himself off. As he did so, none of the other men made to offer him a hand, or barely even glanced at him.

"I am sorry about the table," Stu apologized, while sounding like he meant it. "I ah..." he eyed the three men cautiously. "I tripped, is all. I never was much on my feet."

"He's a real klutz," Slim-Jim agreed.

"Look, the table is fine," Constance waved it down. It wasn't fine, but it was the least of her issues. "It's the noise. You have to remember that I have a full hotel at the moment, and I can't have you lot waking everyone up."

"Waking them?" Piggly-Pete cut in. "It's barely past seven at night."

"I meant in the morning," she continued pointedly. "You leave before the sun rises, and do a good job making sure everyone in town knows it. And then there's the mess you make..." she indicated across the lobby, eyeing what were very obvious, rather obnoxious, muddy-foot prints marking the soft white carpet. They came from the door and led straight to the group of men.

Tex-Mex eyed the footprints, looking rather nonplussed by it. His boots were equally as muddy, as was his entire outfit. Constance's body shook as she suppressed the image of what his room must look like. "It's been a hard day's work," Tex-Mex countered. "Sorry if we, ah, make a little mess. Don't worry, you'll be covered for it." Another wink.

"That's not the..." Constance bit her tongue. These men were rude pigs, but they were also guests. Constance just couldn't bring herself to chastise a guest, regardless of how much they needed it. "Just, try a little harder, please. I would greatly appreciate it."

Tex-Mex smirked, Slim-Jim sneered, and Piggly-Pete frowned. The only one that seemed put-out by the exchange was Stu, who gestured to Constance that he was sorry about the noise. Indeed, standing among those other three men, Stu could not have looked more out of place.

"We've got to be hitting it," Tex-Mex finally said. "Early day tomorrow. But we'll make sure to take your words into account."

"Yeah," Slim-Jim agreed.

"We will do that," Piggly-Pete finished off.

The three men turned on their heel and stampeded across the lobby and toward the stairs. As they went, they tracked mud across the carpet and up the stairs, laughing and carrying on the whole way. Constance watched the three go, counting the seconds until she would be alone so that she could scream into the rooftops.

Behind the three men, Stu hurried along. When he caught them half-way up the stairs, he made to push through them to get to the front, but they wouldn't allow it.

"No ya don't," Tex-Mex snapped as he pushed Stu back. "After what you been sayin' all day."

"Yeah!" Piggly-Pete agreed. "You're lucky we don't push you down the stairs for what you been doing."

"I'm sorry," Stu hurried. "I didn't mean —"

"Yeah, you did," Tex-Mex growled. "Try that again and..." as the four men reached the top of the stairs and turned the corner, their voices faded.

Constance remained where she was, listening as four different doors opened and closed. She then remained standing and listening, able to hear each of the men as they got ready for bed. They were loud. They were obnoxious. They were smelly, dirty and ungrateful. But at least they went to bed early. The only issue now was that they would certainly wake the whole hotel when they woke up at 4am to go to work. She no longer stayed at the hotel overnight, having her own place with Jonas, but she had been told... again and again and again, that they did every other day, so she doubted her little speech tonight would change that.

Alone now, Constance got about cleaning up the mess the four men had made. It was the tenth night in a row that a mess of similar proportions had been left behind and where she should have called in Dakota to clean it, she felt that a mess such as this one needed special attention.

Tex-Mex, Slim-Jim, Piggly-Pete and Stu were four of twenty construction workers that were staying at The Lone Peak Hotel. They had moved in ten days ago, and had at least another three months to go. And where all twenty had their intricacies that annoyed Constance to no end, these four were the worst.

, that's not really fair. Stu was fine. Of the twenty workers that stumbled into the hotel every night and stampeded out every morning, Stu was probably the most polite, and certainly the most quiet. Seeing him in here tonight with this lot caught Constance by surprise, as he was so vastly different. And although they claimed he fell, she had a sneaking suspicion that they pushed him. But that was neither here nor there. The point was that each and every single one of the twenty were a pain in her rear end.

What annoyed Constance the most about her current predicament wasn't just the noise that they made. And it wasn't how ungrateful they were. And it had nothing to do with the next three months that she'd have to put up with it either. The reason that she got so angry every time she saw the construction workers was because they stood as a reminder that change was coming and that The Lone Peak was going to be affected by it.

A bypass was being built around the small town of Modest Peak, one that would cut the town off from the highway entirely. These workers were a handful of the many that had been hired to build the bypass, and where a large portion were staying on site, these lucky few had somehow managed to secure room and board for themselves. She guessed them to be the 'bosses' of their particular field, but she didn't care to speak to them for long enough to confirm this.

It was the bypass that had the majority of Constance's attention. Although she had long since resigned herself to the inevitability of the bypass, knowing there was nothing she could do about it, that didn't mean she had to like it. Having these men staying at the hotel, using it while they literally fast-tracked the demise of the hotel, was akin to being spat at in the face... or at least that was how she saw it.

If only they would keep it down! They were so darn rude! As Constance stacked piles of chipped and broken lumber under her arms, she shuddered at the thought that those men were in charge of anyone, and then got about wondering who was in charge of them.... and what this person had to do to get them to listen. And just like that, a sudden brain wave swept over Constance.

Of course these men had a superior, someone they reported to! Everyone did! She couldn't kick them out of her hotel, and had no intention of it. But what she might be able to do is go behind their back and speak to their boss, see if he could pull them into line. Just the thought of seeing Tex-Mex slink meekly into the hotel tomorrow night, after being reprimanded by his boss, sent a flutter through Constance the likes of which she hadn't felt in ten days.

It took Constance another twenty minutes to clean up the mess left behind by those three men. During this time, more workers returned from the site and added to the mess. But for once, Constance didn't care, heck, she barely noticed. Her thoughts were with tomorrow and what she was going to say to their boss. Oh, how she couldn't wait for that!

Chapter Three

"I refuse to believe that there isn't anything we can do!" Mr. Trunch, the owner of Modest Peak's supermarket, The Lone Aisle, puffed his cheeks out and physically shook as he punched his curled-up fist into his hand. "There has to be something!"

"Hear, hear!" The crowd of ten people cheered along, all nodding their heads as they murmured their agreement.

"My entire business is at stake!" he continued angrily. Mr. Trunch was a stocky figure, with no neck to speak of, and very puffy cheeks. As he spoke, he worked himself up, and as he worked himself up, his face grew redder and redder.

The words that Mr. Trunch shouted were music to the crowd of ten's ears. Everything he said, they agreed with. And with each word spoken, they stamped their feet, clapped their hands, and nodded so furiously that Constance was just waiting for one of their heads to fall from their necks.

It was a Town Hall council meeting that Constance found herself in. All five members of the council were there, along with anyone in town that felt a need to come along and have their opinion heard. Where Constance was a part of the council, and thus obligated to go, she was a little surprised that more people from town hadn't turned up. Ten wasn't very many, not by a long way. She guessed that, like her, the rest of the town had long since resigned themselves to their fate.

What was odd about this council meeting though, was that for once it wasn't called by a member of the council. Instead, it was organized by none other than the Mayor of Denver, Mayor Brumbry.

To Constance, Mayor Brumbry had always reminded her of a Ring Master at a circus. He had a thick handle-bar mustache, wore a silly top hat, a coat that was too large, and shouted rather than spoke. On top of that, he was always trying to argue a point, to sell an angle, to make his word the last one anyone heard. In short, he was a politician.

"I hear what you're saying, Mr. Trunch," Mayor Brumbry spoke up, holding his hands out to soften the crowd. He stood at the front of the room with Constance, and the other three members of the council that had bothered to turn up. The crowd of ten stood huddled a few feet further back, staunching over the council members like a mob waiting for the right time to attack. "And I've already addressed your concern. I was hoping for some new questions?"

"New questions!" Mr. Trunch blasted. "You're not getting no new questions! It's just the one statement, the same one we been hollering since day one! We don't want the bypass!" The crowd erupted with cheers and salutations, clapping their hands and stamping their feet in agreement.

The council meeting had been called to discuss the bypass, for what must have been the fifth time since it had been announced. When it was first announced well over a month previously, the reaction was appropriately morose. No one in town wanted the thing, as they were all well aware of how it would affect business. With no traffic passing through on a daily basis, small businesses would suffer.

Unfortunately, all the complaining in the world didn't make any difference, and as the people of Modest Peak shouted, the bypass went ahead into the planning stages until now when it was well and truly into construction. The only difference between this town meeting and the others was that the Mayor of Denver had decided to come all the way to Modest Peak to try and... well, Constance wasn't sure.

Mayor Brumbry was visibly flustered, and becoming more so by the second. No doubt he had expected a little anger, and maybe some argument... but this was something else. The crowd was turning on him and might very soon start tearing him limb from limb.

"I... there isn't anything... it's happening!" he shouted the crowd down without success.

Mayor Brumbry didn't have to come to Modest Peak at all. He had nothing to do with the small mountain town. Denver was well over two hours away after all. But the bypass was a part of his campaign promise to the voters in Denver and no doubt he came to Modest Peak as part of an insurance policy, to make sure that they didn't do anything silly.

"That's not good enough!" It was Mr. Buck shouting now. "This bypass will cripple me! And who's going to by me badges?! You?!!!!" He shook his hand in anger at Mayor Brumbry, glaring at the poor man like he wanted to kill him... which he very well might.

Mr. Buck was the local weirdo. A hermit by nature, he looked to be anywhere between fifty and one hundred years old, with a bent back, a club foot that he claimed to have gotten in the war – although he never did say which war – and skin so saggy that Constance could see it hanging off his bones. Even the act of shaking his fist seemed to tire him.

"Your badges?" Mayor Brumbry asked with exasperation. "What are you —"

"Me badges!" Mr. Buck shouted again. "I be making badges for tourists, selling them from me wagon. It's how I feed myself. So, I ask you again, who is going to buy them now that we don't be getting no more tourists?!"

"I don't know how to..." Mayor Brumbry had started sweating. It poured from his brow and despite how much he wiped at it, it seemed to do little good.

"We moved here three months ago and now we're going to have to move again!" Dakota and her twin brother, Dexter stepped to the front of the group. "Who is going to pay our moving costs? Not to mention the friends we've made!"

Dakota worked for Constance, and had already been told by Constance that the bypass wouldn't affect her job. But she didn't seem to care, or understand. As for Dexter, he worked for Jonas as a tour guide and ranger, having been hired thanks to Dakota and Constance. Like his sister, he was vague, constantly spaced out, and a little slow when it came to most things.

"I only just finished up my training!" Dexter complained. It looked as if he was on the verge of tears and Dakota took his hand and gave the back of it a kiss. It was strange, seeing as they were brother and sister, but no stranger than anything else that Constance had seen that night. "I can't train somewhere else – I won't!"

The meeting was starting to get out of hand, and then some. As Mayor Brumbry did his best to try and calm the people down, they seemed to grow louder and angrier. And although Constance didn't think any of them were capable of physical harm... things did happen.

Really, this was all Mayor Brumbry's fault. He had called Constance two days earlier and asked for her to set this meeting up, so that he could 'alleviate fears' as he had put it. Constance had tried to tell him it would do no good, and nothing he said would alleviate anyone's fears. But being the politician that he was, he was convinced that wouldn't be the case. Based on the way he was currently sweating, and shaking, and trembling, she guessed he was wishing he'd taken her advice.

"Ms. Aberfield..." Mayor Brumbry turned to Constance and indicated for her to take over. Really, it was more akin to begging than anything else. She was certain that if she had said 'no,' he just might have broken into tears. "Please?"

The small crowd was beginning to gain momentum. With every complaint made, they seemed to grow in strength and resolve. Although the bypass had already begun, and nothing would stop it, Constance wouldn't have been surprised if this group of ten people turned on their heel, marched to the site and started tearing up the roadworks themselves. And it was because of this, and only this, that she decided it was time to step in.

"If everybody could calm down for just a second!" Constance shouted over the noise. "Please!"

The effect wasn't instantaneous, but it was close enough. The grumbling lessened, the shouting dissipated and the clapping of hands and stamping of feet slowly faded until it was quite enough that Constance could hear herself think for a change.

"Thank you," Mayor Brumbry sighed. "Now if you would all just —"

"I don't think so." Constance held her finger up to silence the man. She knew that nothing he said could help the matter, and would likely only make it worse. "You've said enough, I think." She then turned back to face the crowd. "Now, no doubt all of you are upset —"

"And more than that!" Mr. Buck hollered to applause.

"Yes, yes," Constance silenced them again. "And you have every right to be. But, unfortunately, being upset isn't going to change anything."

"What then?" Mr. Trunch shouted to more applause. "What will?!"

"Please, Constance! You've got to help!" Dexter pleaded. As he did, Dakota held onto his arm, nodding along.

"Well?!" Mr. Buck finished for the crowd.

All eyes were on Constance, waiting with baited breath. Surely, she had a response. Surely, she had a way to solve this calamity. Surely, she had called this town hall because she had a plan and she needed them to help her put it into action. Surely, Constance Aberfield was going to save the day?

"There's nothing we can do," she sighed, looking down at her feet as she spoke. She was so darn regretful, and embarrassed, that she couldn't even meet the crowd's eyes. "Nothing at all."

It was the cold hard truth, and one that Constance had long since resigned herself to. When the bypass had first been announced, she hadn't been as angry as everyone else, but like them she was sure that it would ruin her business and the town in general. But the more she looked into it, the more she came to realize that there was nothing she could do. The only thing she could do was accept that change was inevitable and try and adapt.

"You don't mean that!" Mr. Trunch gasped in shock.

"Constance?" Dexter and Dakota both exclaimed, their eyes bulging in surprise.

"I do," she affirmed, nodding her head once as she did so. "I've looked into it and there isn't... this is out of our reach. It's a Denver program and unfortunately, they don't have much time for us small town folk." She bowed her head, hoping that her show of acceptance would help ease the people. It did not.

The next ten to fifteen minutes was spent by the ten town members shouting, yelling and screaming their dismay. None wanted to believe what Constance had said, and each one wanted to get their complaint out in the air before they were even willing to listen to reason.

And even then, once it was all said and done, the complaints continued as the people slowly shuffled from the room and back onto the street. Not a single one had gotten what they wanted, or anything close to it. Constance could only imagine what they might do now.

"Thank you for that, Mrs. Aberfield," Mayor Brumbry said once the room had quietened down and everyone had begun to leave. "That was... it was getting a little out of hand. Who knew that such a small town could produce such a vibrant kind of -"

"Mayor Brumbry," Constance cut in politely, even offering him a smile as she did.

"Yes?" he asked, smiling back, leaning forward, eager to hear what she had to say.

"Will you please, please, just keep your mouth shut, turn around and leave. Right now, would be good." She was all smiles, even blinking a few times as she indicated the door.

Mayor Brumbry looked appropriately surprised and put out by Constance's polite – although very rude – offer. But he didn't argue, or deny her. He seemed to realize that he was the villain in this little showing, and figured that it would be best to leave before anything bad happened. He had won after all, so there was no need to hang around and gloat.

And as Constance watched him go, she couldn't help but feel dirty, like she needed a bath. Although she was right in saying that there was nothing she could do about the bypass, and laying down and accepting it was the only reasonable course of action to take, it didn't mean that she was going to feel good about it. In fact, the complete opposite was true.

Constance Aberfield hated change, but she was beginning to realize that it was inevitable as an approaching storm. Constance's only real hope, and that of the entire town of Modest Peak, was to adapt to the change and hope that she came out the other side unscathed. That was the nature of the beast, after all.

Chapter Four

The high-way bypass of Modest Peek was a rather large job, at least from what Constance could tell. Starting some ten miles out from Modest Peak itself, it ran for well over fifty miles, was comprised of over eight full lanes, four bridges, one underpass, required acres upon acres of trees chopped down, landed flattened and a whole host of others things done that Constance didn't even begin to understand. And what was more, it was all to happen over a period of three and a half months

The morning after the town hall meeting, Constance made her way out to the bypass, heading for where she was sure she'd find the site's foreman. When the bypass had first started up, a series of construction trailers had set up at the start of the construction, and from what she understood, the foreman was staying in one of these. She hadn't called to tell him she was coming, figuring that if she just turned up she might catch him off-guard and be able to use that to her advantage.

As she drove to foreman's trailer, she was plagued with memories of the previous night, all the yelling, and shouting and carrying on. She could see the pained faces of the townspeople, people she called friends, and the disappointment on their faces when she told them there was nothing to be done. Oh, how dreadful!

But it was the truth. There wasn't anything that could be done. Some things were bigger than Modest Peak, and this bypass was one of them. Indeed, as she turned off what was still the main-highway, and caught her first glimpse of the bypass, she realized just how right she was. The darn thing was gigantic.

As a girl, Constance and her father used to make weekly trips out to this part of the country. Once upon a time, it was acres and acres of dense forest, filled to the brim with wildlife and nature reserves. Now it was hardly recognizable, if at all! The trees had been cleared, the land had been flattened and Constance didn't even want to think about what had happened to the wildlife that used to live there.

She kept her eyes dead ahead, ignoring the machinery that plowed through the few remaining trees, and the slabs of concrete that were slowly being stacked and built upon. She wasn't here to try and stop the by-pass. She was here to try and curtail the habits of her guests, and that was what she was going to do.

As such, she steered her car along the cleared roadway and toward the set of trailers at the very start of the construction. A few questions, and a little nagging saw her pointed toward the foreman's office and a few moments later she was sitting in the small office, waiting for the return of the foreman.

It was only now that Constance was able to take a moment and think about what she was going to say, and ask for. She had been so darn distracted with what had happened the previous night that she'd barely given it a thought. Sure, she was going to ask if he could have a word with his workers about proper hotel etiquette. But it was how she was going to ask that had her thinking. Was she going to demand outright, or try and sweeten the man up before making her demands? Really, it all depended on the foreman himself and the kind of man he was. Once Constance got her first reading of him, then she would decide a course of action.

And so, she waited, and waited and waited. Five minutes turned to ten and ten turned to twenty. After thirty minutes, she considered leaving, but then decided that was what he wanted. After forty minutes she considered leaving a note, but then stopped herself. And then, after a full hour of waiting, the foreman finally stumbled into his office.

"Hello?" he blinked back his surprise at the sight of Constance. "And you are?"

She was immediately put on the back foot. She had told the workers to inform him that she was waiting, but clearly they hadn't done that. This whole operation was a shamble. "My name is Constance Aber —"

"I don't care for your name," he waved her down as he strode into the office. Barely looking at her, he went to his desk and started shuffling through piles of work papers. "What are you doing here? You're from that town... what's it called – Modest Peak?"

Foreman Joe was your typical, burly, brutish, all bravado, kind of construction worker. In that small trailer, he appeared twice the size of Constance, with shoulders so wide and a waist so narrow that he looked like an upside-down triangle. Everything about Foreman Joe suggested that he wasn't the kind of guy that one spoke down to. And yet, Constance didn't care.

It was his off-handish, downright rude dismissal of her before she had so much as said two words, that first lit the fire underneath Constance. But it was the way he talked down about Modest Peak, her home! that really set the fire ablaze.

"Listen here! My name is Constance Aberfield, and it's a name you better – will you stand still!" It wasn't a scream, but it was about as close as it came to one. As Constance tried to put Foreman Joe in his place, he barely paid her attention, if any at all. He was across the room, rifling through filing boxes and pulling out blueprints. Not so much as looking at Constance.

"Don't take it personal, love." Constance's eyes bulged, but he carried one without a pause. "You've caught me at a bad time here. My freaking Chief Surveyor hasn't been seen since the start of day." He strode back across the room, parking himself over his table as he flipped through a larger folder – back to Constance. "So, spare me your complaints, or list of reasons this here bypass has to stop. I'll tell you that I'll consider your opinion, you go on your way, and this thing here gets built anyway. How's that?" Head down, his eyes scanning down a page he'd landed on. Constance got the sense she could have started dancing, and he wouldn't have noticed her.

"I'm not here to complain." She stepped around to the side of the table, trying to put herself in his field of view. "I'm the owner of the hotel your men are staying at – some of your men."

"They're not my men," he mumbled without looking up.

"What? Yes, they are. You are Joe the Fore —"

"What I meant was, they work for me. Yes. But what they do outside of this place is on them. I do not care at all."

For one of the first times in her life, Constance was speechless. This man, this brute, this orcish human being, was impossible! Like trying to wear down a stone with water, she sensed there wasn't much she could do to get him to listen to her.

Suddenly, Foreman Joe's eyes lit up and he snatched up the paper he was reading. Holding it up so as to better read it, he half turned his body as if to make for the door – the only door. It was in that moment, that Constance saw her chance. As Foreman Joe double checked what he had picked up, she darted for the doorway, planting herself firmly in it. And then, hands on hips, legs spread, she cocked a smile and waited.

Foreman Joe noticed her a second later. As his eyes finished on the page, he took a step toward the door, looked up, saw Constance standing there, and quickly pulled himself to a halt. Constance could feel the entire trailer shake at the force of his giant strides coming to a sudden standstill.

"I don't – what are you doing?" Foreman Joe asked dumbly, looking at Constance as if he had never seen a woman standing in a doorway before.

"You're not leaving this room until you listen to what I came here to say." She spread her legs a little wider, making sure to meet his eyes with her determined stare.

"Huh?" Foreman Joe tilted his head in confusion. He then rolled his eyes, took one long step toward Constance, reached out to literally shove her out of the way and —

"Don't you touch me!" Constance shouted as she slapped his hand down, her body tensing up. "Touch me and I'll scream." She held her hand up as if to slap his away again. And all the while she fixed him with an unblinking, 'don't even think about it' kind of stare.

Foreman Joe clenched his jaw and fists both, looking like he was ready to start smashing at the ground like a giant ape. But reason quickly took back over as he assessed the situation, realized he was trapped, and proceeded accordingly. "What do you want?" he asked bluntly as his body relaxed.

"To speak to you about four of your workers staying at my hotel."

"I told you they're not —"

"They work for you, don't they? How about you show some managerial zeal and discipline your men. Especially where it is warranted." Constance knew she had a small window until this man's patience was tested and he would just shove her out of the way. She thought it best to really hammer home her advantage while she had the chance.

Foreman Joe fumed. "Which ones? What did they do?"

"I don't know they're actual... Slim-Jim?" she waited for a sign of acknowledgment. A quick nod from Foreman Joe confirmed it. "Piggly-Pete, Tex-Mex and Stu. All four have been nothing but menaces the past ten nights and I'd like you to have a talk with them."

"Stu?" Foreman Joe asked, eyebrow raised. "Surveyor Stu?"

"Well, I don't know his moniker... small man? Hideous comb-over and overbite?"

"Look. Those three... they're gonna be menaces anywhere they go. That's just who they are. I'll have a chat with 'em, but don't expect much. And as for Stu? I don't think you're going to be needing to worry about him no more."

"What? Why?"

"As of this morning, Stu is MIA."

The shock nearly knocked Constance off of her feet. But instead, it just stunned her. Her eyes turned to dinner plates, her mouth hung agape and her eyebrows disappeared beneath her bangs. Stu was missing. What did that mean? For how long? How did he know —

"Hey!" Constance stumbled and tripped to the side as Foreman Joe, taking advantage of her trance-like state, pushed her out of the way and stepped out from the trailer.

It took Constance a few extra seconds to recover. But the second she was back on her feet, and back in the room in general, she turned on her heel and hurried out of the trailer and after Foreman Joe. She simply had to know what was going on.

Foreman Joe was less than fifteen feet from the trailer when Constance flew from its door. The moment she spotted him, she hurried in beside him, keeping pace as he picked his own up to escape her.

"What do you want now?" he barked. He took a quick turn, nearly doubling back the other way in an effort to throw Constance. But it was no good. She simply followed suit, having to sprint to keep up.

"What do you mean that Stu has disappeared? How – did he not turn up to work?"

"Na, he turned up like always. But that was five hours ago, and no one has seen him since – will you stop following me!" Foreman Joe came to a dead-halt as he turned on Constance, towering over her like some sort of monster. Indeed, the exclamation was so loud that half the workers within earshot stopped what they were doing so as to watch the confrontation

Constance didn't balk. She barely even blinked. Hands on her hip, doing her best to appear almost bored, she lazily looked up at Foreman Joe as she said, "Got that out of your system, have we?" Foreman Joe deflated, and Constance carried on. "Can you please just give me a straight answer. Do that and I will stop following you."

"Fine," Foreman Joe exhaled. "One question."

"Why are you so certain that he's disappeared and not just... oh, I don't know? Gone for a walk or something like that? You seem awfully certain that you won't be seeing him again."

Foreman Joe smirked and shook his head. "If you knew anything about Stu, you'd know that barely an hour goes past without him at my heels, complaining about something. Two hours and no Stu, that's odd. Three is unheard of. We're at five now and... and I'd believe pigs could talk before I'd believe something wasn't wrong. You get me?"

She got him, all right. Desperate to ask another question, but knowing it would do no good, Constance offered a reserved nod instead. This was all Foreman Joe needed and less than a second later he was powering down the new bypass, as far away from Constance as possible.

Constance was glad for it. There was something odd about what she had just been told, and she needed a moment to process it. Her gut was tingling, which always meant that something was going on. A few moments of silence was in order so that she could start to make sense of —

The noise of the work site was incredible, and it was only just now, that she had a moment to herself, that Constance really took notice. From the bulldozers, to the chainsaws, to the mixers, to the trucks, to the sounds of men yelling at other men, it was a smorgasbord of loud noises specifically designed to distract Constance and drown out all thoughts.

For a moment, Constance considered hurrying back to her car. It was time she headed back anyway, and she could use the drive to start thinking about this Stu disappearance. Odds were that it was nothing... but her gut disagreed. She turned in the direction of her car, when she noticed a collection of trees across the bypass road, unharmed by the roadworks.

It was small forest, backing onto what other states might call a mountain, but here in Colorado, it barely warranted being called a rocky-hill. Constance recognized the location instantly, it being one that she and her father used to go to when she was a child.

Overtaken by a sudden urge to explore, to revisit the past in a time where she was constantly being urged to join the future, Constance hurried across the road and into the forest. Silence enveloped her the second she breached the trees, as if the thick foliage and dense forestry were able to silence the outside completely. And as soon as she was within the small forest, Constance felt overcome with a sense of nostalgia.

She recognized the place like she hadn't been gone a day. Feeling a sense of excitement, she hurried through the forest toward where it backed onto the hill. There, she knew of a large quarry that used to have a deep pool in the center. She doubted that it still existed... but she hoped.

The quarry was still there. Constance clapped her hands together with excitement as she breached the small quarry. It was no larger than her hotel in diameter, with a pool in the center smaller than most private swimming pools. The only thing being that there was no water in the pool.

And yet, Constance couldn't take her eyes from it.... but not for the reason one might think. She stepped further into the clearing, and as she reached the edges of the quarry, where the land gave way into the pool, she crouched down and climbed into the hollow base. Her eyes the whole time were planted on the very center of the pool, in the dirt.

She had almost missed it, but now that she was close up, less than five feet away, there could be no doubt. A human hand, was sticking straight up from beneath the dirt. That hand connected itself to an arm, and that arm to a body. A dead body. And although Constance didn't recognize the hand, she had no doubt that the body it belonged to was Stu's.

Chapter Five

For all the things that were changing in Constance's life at this moment in time, she was at least able to take some solace in the fact that one thing hadn't changed: she was a magnet when it came to finding dead bodies. Seriously! If there was a dead body in the area, chances were that Constance was going to find it. She just hoped that when her time came, there wasn't anything nefarious about it, and her body didn't wind up being hidden. If that did happen, she wouldn't be there to find it. She'd be dead!

The moment that Constance breached the quarry, she knew something was wrong. She could sense it. And when she spied that hand in the center of the dried-up pool – even though it was too small and far away to properly see – she knew what it was. Some might say that the odds of her finding that dead body after only just learning about Stu's disappearance were astronomical, but for Constance it was just a day in the life.

And it was Stu, too, the dead body. Once she spotted the hand, Constance hurried back out of the forest to a spot where her cell phone got reception. She then made the necessary calls and waited. It was a process she was used to by now, sitting back while the proper authorities got about their business. Ambulances came, fire trucks turned up, the entire Modest Peak police force made sure to stop by. Even a few locals, who must have seen the commotion as it passed through town, hurried out to the site. No doubt the entire town would be speaking of this tonight.

It was about an hour after the police arrived and began fencing off the site, that Constance came to a rather remarkable decision and one that was certainly a sign of growth: she decided to go home. Ordinarily, she would hang around for hours as she tried to insert herself into the case, to try and convince the sheriff that she was going to be working the case with him. Ordinarily, the site of a dead body and the idea of a case to work would have had Constance's entire body tingling with anticipation. But not this time.

For whatever reason, Constance just had no urge to work it. It might have been because she didn't know Stu personally, or anyone else that may have been involved. It might have been the lack of personal stakes in the case. Or it might have just been age getting to Constance and a desire to take a hot bath, rather than sit around in the dirt waiting for the police, only to be dismissed on sight. Whatever the reason, Constance was done.

As such, she felt a small thrill when she climbed back into her car and took off back toward the Lone Peak. She didn't even bother telling the sheriff, sure that he would be too preoccupied with digging up the body to worry about her. This was definitely the right decision. With the theme of change in mind, she liked to think that this was a good sign. She was growing as a person, adapting to the new world.

So divorced from the case was Constance that she barely gave it a second thought as she drove home. In her mind, the case was pretty clear cut. One of the workers from the sight had evidently gotten into a fight with Stu, killed him by mistake, and then buried the body. A little grilling would have him confessing and that would be that. Really, there was no need for her to get involved at all.

When she arrived back at the hotel, she wasn't surprised to find it empty... although she was a little annoyed. Her two best workers, Sydney and Eleanor were both on holidays, which was half the reason that Dakota had been hired in the first place. But the woman was nowhere to be seen! Constance tried calling her cell, but it went straight to voice mail. As such, she was forced to work the reception for two whole hours until Dakota finally came back.

"I'm sorry, I'm sorry," she blustered as she charged into the lobby of the hotel like a bull from the gate. "I was in Denver with Dexter. We had a karaoke competition we've been prepping for all month! We find out tomorrow how we did. Isn't that exciting!"

Constance wasn't listening, not a single word. Instead she waited until Dakota had stopped speaking and then told her to stick to the desk like glue while she went upstairs and took a bath – one she had been craving for hours! She had dirt all up her legs and in her shoes and relished in the idea of getting rid of it. And sure, she should have just gone home to take the bath, but she still liked doing it at the hotel when she could. To her, there was just something about it. A feeling of being home.

As the water poured from the faucet and into the tub, Constance slipped into her fluffy-purple bathrobe. She could feel the heat radiating from the water, filling the room, already working its way toward relaxing her. She wasn't in the bath yet, but she was glad in her choice of this over working that stupid, sure to be solved quickly, case —

"Constance!" The heat from the room seemed to evaporate as the call, coming from downstairs and in the lobby, shook the room. "Constance! I'm coming up!"

Constance thought quickly. She turned the water off, even though the bath was only half full, and then dipped her foot in, "Ow!" she yelped as the water burned her toes. Grimacing, she hurriedly turned on the cold water to try and even it out. And all the while she could hear footsteps, hurrying down the hall and toward her.

"Constance!" the familiar voice called. "I'm coming in!"

"Don't!" she called back over her shoulder. She shut the cold water off and tested the bath again. It was freezing! "I'm in the tub, Rog!"

"I need to speak to you!" he was right at the door now, no doubt waiting until she gave the signal to come in.

"I'm... can you come back later?" Still in her bathrobe, she stood over the tub, half poised to climb in.

"I'd rather not. This is really, really important."

Constance felt her stomach sink as she looked to the half-filled tub. She had been so close to getting in, so close to sinking into the depths of the hot water and putting this day behind her. So darn close! "Fine!" she shouted as she stepped back from the tub. "Come in —"

The door flew open and Sheriff Nevil flew into the small bathroom. A large man – wide in shoulder and tall in height – the room seemed to shrink in size as his hulking frame filled the space. Indeed, he almost had to tilt his head so as not to scrape it along the ceiling. Regardless of this, one look at Constance in her bathrobe and he burst into laughter. "Nice robe!" he cackled.

"What do you want!?" she snapped as she made to pull the robe tighter around her bodice. "Can't you see I'm busy."

Constance and Sheriff Nevil had known one another their entire lives. Both born in Modest Peak, they went to the same schools, worked similar day jobs, and remained friends right up until now... a friendship that was on thin ice if Sheriff Nevil didn't stop smirking. Even when Constance started trying her hand at amateur sleuthing, Sheriff Nevil and she had remained good friends, despite the fact that he tried to foil her at every turn.

"I'm surprised you're here?" Sheriff Nevil continued, grinning like a school boy the whole while. "I thought you be on your hands and knees, digging through piles of dirt in search of clues."

"Maybe you don't know me half as well as you think you do?" she said pointedly. "If you did, you would know that stopping me from taking this much-needed bath is the last thing you should be —"

"Constance, can we be serious for a moment?" The humor dropped from his voice, replaced with a serious, almost morbid tenor. "As hard as it might be to believe, I didn't come here to catch you in your night dress."

There was no need for Sheriff Nevil to explain, for Constance already knew what he was going to say. It was the same thing he said every time a new case arrived, one that he didn't want her working. No doubt he had an argument already in his head, lain out and ready to fire away with when she tried to intervene. Lucky then that she planned on saving him this arduous task.

"Keep it to yourself," she said. "I know what you're here to ask, and I'm pleased to say that I will not be working the case. Or trying to, for that matter. Happy?"

Sheriff Nevil blinked back his surprise, clearly caught off guard. "You're not?"

"No, I'm not," she confirmed. "Honestly, I don't even know why you would think that I'd try." That was a laugh, and Constance made sure not to be looking at Sheriff Nevil when she said it.

"Silly me," he chuckled. "Well, you're right, I came here to ask – beg if I had to. Please don't work the case, Constance. This one time, please don't —"

"What did I just say?" she snapped. "I have no interest."

"None?"

"Not a modicum."

"Oh... good... great." Sheriff Nevil sort of swayed back and forth, twiddling his thumbs and looking over Constance's shoulder as if at something on the wall. He had something else to say.

"Spit it out!"

"Mayor Brumbry is going to come and visit you. And he's going to try and convince you to work this case for him."

Now it was Constance's turn to act surprised. "Mayor Brumbry – what? Why? Why on earth would he —"

"I've shut the bypass down until this case is solved. No work is to be done on it at all. Now, I've told the Mayor that this case is my top priority and I'll be putting my best men on it, but that didn't seem to be enough."

Constance beamed. She blushed. She made sure to make her pleasure as obvious as possible. "Well, you can hardly blame him for wanting the best —"

"He doesn't want the best. He wants you," Sheriff Nevil chided. "And I told him that you're not a cop, but he's read your books and that piece in the Denver Times, and seems to think there isn't a case you can't solve." Constance had written several best-selling books, each one revolving around a case she had worked. She had also been subject to a 'portrait' in the Denver Times, one aimed at 'uncovering' the truth behind the amateur sleuth. She was glad to hear that her fame was spreading.

"I'm glad to see there's a politician living that's willing to tell the truth every now and —"

"Constance!" Sheriff Nevil towered over her, eyes pleading as he looked down from his perch. "Please, can you promise me that when the mayor comes, you won't take the case? Please!"

She had no intention of taking the case. None. But still, it was nice to pretend that she might. As such, Constance took her time deliberating, making sure to 'um' and 'ah' for as long as possible. She could see it wearing on Sheriff Nevil too, breaking him down, really grinding him to the floor. And then, when he looked just about ready to snap, she finished with an "OK, I won't take it."

Sheriff Nevil had never looked so happy, and she was quite sure that was she not wearing a bathrobe, he would have hugged her. "Thank you," he admitted. "Now, doesn't that feel better?"

"It does," she agreed. "Now, can I please take my bath in peace?"

"What?" A sly smile from the Sheriff. "Don't you want to ask me about the case anyway? Come on... I know you're dying to find out some more."

Constance shrugged. "What's there to find out? One of the workers killed Stu and tried to bury the body. If it were me – which it isn't. I'd grill the lot of them until one folded. Really, even if I wanted to work the case there wouldn't be time. Any decent cop would have it finished by sundown."

It was a purposeful stab at Sheriff Nevil, and one he took gracefully. His entire body shook from withheld laughter and his grin was such that it split his face in two. "As always, Constance, your analysis is not bad. I've got the entire crew at the station now, already in the midst of being interrogated. We've got a list of those he was closest to, the last people he was seen with, and a timetable that should tell us where each crew member was around the time of death. Like you said, simple."

There was a moment's pause after this revelation, and Constance was only too aware of its reason. Sheriff Nevil was after her opinion. He would never admit it, and would rather die before saying as such, but the reason he had just lain out his m.o. so cleanly for her, the reason he was here in the first place, was for her approval. He wanted to make sure he was on the right track, or that there wasn't something he was missing.

And yes, Sheriff Nevil would never, ever, ever say such a thing, but Constance knew him as well as she knew herself. She knew him so well in fact, that to call him out for this would only be reductive and all together pointless. So, she didn't.

"Sounds good," she managed as she tried her hardest not to smile. "That's what I would do." It was too. A simple case meant a simple process.

"Perfect!" Sheriff Nevil clapped his hands together and made to leave the small bathroom. "And please, Constance, when the Mayor does come around, which he will, say no. Please."

"I'm already working on my rejection letter," she joked. "Now, go away. It's time for a much-needed bath, to which you are not invited."

This got Sheriff Nevil laughing as he exited the room, and closed the door behind him. Once he was gone, and the door was locked, Constance finally got about finishing up the bath. And then, when it was good and ready, she slid into the warm depths of the water, losing herself in the heat, the steam and the all-around goodness that a perfectly run bath had to offer.

Not once did the case of Stu and the buried body come to mind either. She had told Sheriff Nevil that she wasn't interested, and it was the truth. Constance was a changed woman.

Chapter Six

Constance's bath went for a little longer than she had originally intended... possibly a few hours longer. There was even a chance that she had fallen asleep, if only for a few minutes. By the time she climbed from the tub, the water was cold, her skin was wrinkled, and she was impossibly relaxed.

It was easily the most relaxed she had felt in months, like she was floating on a cloud. Indeed, she seemed to glide above the floor as she exited the bathroom, swept down the hallway and descend down the stairs and into the foyer. Her eyes were just about closed, but her feet knew where they were going. It was amazing what a good bath could do, paired with a total lack of worry. Her mood was peaked, and it was going to stay that way... and then she opened her eyes.

There were two things she noticed when she first opened her eyes and took in the hotel lobby. The first was the mess. Dark, muddy footprints traced their way from the door and through the lobby. There were dozens of them, turning her nice white carpet to a dull brown. As well as that, there were boots piled by the door, jackets thrown across pieces of furniture and a smell that she couldn't quite put her finger on. No doubt the workers were back from their interrogations, and no doubt Foreman Joe hadn't spoken to them.

The second thing she noticed was Mayor Brumbry, sitting on the couch, knee bobbing up and down as he waited, top hat spinning in his hands. At the sight of Constance walking down the stairs and into the lobby, he leaped to his feet and ran for her like she was a life source that he was desperate to get his hands upon.

"Ms. Aberfield!" he cried as he hurried. "Thank the Gods!"

When Constance had first met the mayor, he had reminded her of a circus performer; the ring master to be precise. From his round, red-tinted face, to his constant, over the top smile and the way his hands flew about as he spoke, he was a showman through and through. At the moment, these qualities seemed to be in overdrive, so much so that he was nearly dancing with energy as he reached her.

"Mayor Brumbry," Constance responded casually as she swept past him and made for the doorway. There were eight pairs of boots, tossed into the corner without rhyme or reason. She got about sorting and stacking them... even though this wasn't where boots were kept! "What a pleasant surprise," she finished.

"I need to speak to you." He hovered over her shoulder as she stacked the boots, his hands twisting his top hat nearly in half. "And I need you to keep an open mind when I —"

"The answer is no." She stood straight up and turned to face Mayor Brumbry, meeting his panic-stricken stare with her own determined one. "I know why you're here, and I am sorry, but I have to decline."

"How can you – Sheriff Nevil has already stopped by?" He clenched his fists, bending the hat, and cursed under his breath.

"That's neither here nor there." She strode past the mayor and toward reception where she had started keeping a spare bucket of water, a rag, a scrubbing brush and some cleaning supplies. Ten days in a row of messy footprints to clean had taught her to do so.

"You have to reconsider!" Mayor Brumbry pleaded as he danced around her. "I need this case solved. The Sheriff has closed the darn bypass down until the case is either wrapped up, or abandoned. But there's no chance of it being abandoned for months – and that's assuming that there are no leads! I need this bypass finished!"

Constance made sure to keep her back to him as he begged, so as to emphasize her lack of concern in his plea. "Exactly. You need it finished. To be perfectly frank, it's in my best interest to not work the case." She hadn't thought of it like that before, but now that she did, it made perfect sense.

"What if I made it worth your interest." Constance was on her knees, scrubbing at the stains, so he dropped to his knees too so as to meet her eyes. "I can do that, you know?"

"Bribery?" she scoffed. "I thought you were better than that."

"Bribery?" he exclaimed in shock. "Not I! I was simply going to imply... I was thinking of putting out a reward anyhow, for any information that might wrap this case up! That's all."

"If that's the case, then I hardly see how I might be interested in —"

"What do you need?" he blurted. Still on his knees, he was practically crawling now so as to keep by her side. "Anything!"

"I don't know why you need me?" Bent over, scrubbing as hard as she could, Constance couldn't help but feel a small thrill. Oh, how she loved being told that she was the best. "We have a perfectly good police force here in Modest Peak."

"I've read all your books. I know how good you are – and yes, yes, the Modest Peak police force is perfectly adequate. But again, I cannot emphasize how imperative it is that this bypass get completed, and to schedule. Any help you could bring would be beyond beneficial."

"I'm afraid the answer is no." She hadn't looked at him once during his entire spiel, making sure to keep her attention on the carpet stains... which were starting to disappear. "I'm sorry, Mayor Brumbry, but that's the way it's going to be."

"You're sure?" he begged. "There isn't anything I can do to change your mind? Anything?!"

"I'm afraid not."

Mayor Brumbry was about to give in. He was about to throw in the towel, get to his feet and trudge outside and into the cold. And Constance was about to let go a sigh of relief. She felt a little proud of herself at having turned Mayor Brumbry down. But then, as if fate had decided to intervene, the front door to the hotel flew open and in walked Mayor Brumbry's trump card... not that he even knew of it.

Tex-Mex, Slim-Jim and Piggly-Pete all stumbled into the hotel and through the lobby. From the smell of them, they had just returned from a drink or two at the bar next door, but that wasn't what had Constance gaping in open shock, disgust and downright anger. It was the mud! Their shoes and pants were caked in the stuff and as they walked through the foyer, stepping over Constance as they made for the stairs, they trailed mud over the freshly cleaned carpet, up the stairs and down the hall.

Constance's entire body shook as she watched her clean carpet get re-muddied. She clenched her jaw, she squeezed her fist and for the smallest amount of time, she considered picking up her bucket of water, taking it to Tex-Mex's room and dumping it over him.

"The bypass is closed down, you say?" she asked Mayor Brumbry through gritted teeth.

Mayor Brumbry, for all his faults, was still a politician, and it took him all of a second to see his advantage and press it. "That's right. Could be months. And I do believe that the crew will be remaining here, in Modest Peak, until well after that. But who knows, you might grow to like them?"

Constance still hadn't so much as looked at Mayor Brumbry, but she could sense the grin on his round face. He had found his method of seduction.

"Okay..." Constance nodded slowly as she shuffled across the floor and toward the muddy footprints. "I'll help."

"You will?!" he beamed as he jumped to his feet, put his hat back on his head, and clapped his hands. "Perfect! Now, the first thing I was thinking was... what are you doing?"

Constance was still on her hands and knees, scrubbing at the muck. "I'm cleaning," she said dismissively. "And then I have to take another bath, and then a good night's sleep will be in order, I think."

"But the case —"

"Can wait for tomorrow. Trust me, Mayor Brumbry. I am the professional here."

Constance didn't want to work the case. Truly, she had no urge. But this wasn't about working the case and solving a murder. This was about getting those heathens out of her hotel as soon as possible.

To achieve that, there wasn't much she wouldn't do. Her only regret was how Sheriff Nevil was going to take this sudden change in direction... but it wasn't much of a regret, really. In all likelihood, she'd probably enjoy telling him just as much as she would enjoy seeing the backs of those workers the day they finally left.

And so it was that Constance kept her back to Mayor Brumbry as she scrubbed at the floor and he exited the hotel. Something told her that working with him was going to end in giving her a far bigger headache than any amount of mess or noise ever could, but she didn't worry about that for now. Tonight was for cleaning, tomorrow she would finally start working the case.

Chapter Seven

Constance took the afternoon and the night off, before diving into the case the following morning. She did this for several reasons, the main one being that she assumed this case would be a quick solve and didn't warrant her full attention. Even though she wasn't working the case, her thoughts were still with it. And as she ate her dinner that night, read her book, chatted happily with her husband, and got ready for bed, the case was burrowed in the back of her mind, pressing against her frontal lobe, forcing its way into the fore of her thoughts.

But again, she really didn't give it too much thought, and again, that was just because she assumed it was going to be a rather easy solve. So easy, she assumed, that she felt nearly zero guilt about going against her promise to Sheriff Nevil.

What she did think upon, whenever the case managed to push itself into her frame of mind, was motive: both her own, and that of the murderer.

Her own motive was rather selfish, and not something she was proud of. She wanted the workers gone from her hotel as quick as possible, and was willing to do whatever it took. She hoped that the case would be as simple as she suspected, but she also knew she couldn't take that risk. If there was even a chance that it was more complex than it seemed, she wanted to be there. Oh, how she was already looking forward to the day that the bypass was done with and she was finally able to see the back of those animals.

The motive of the murderer was far more complex. And if not complex, at the very least it was unknown. Whenever she did spare a moment to think on the case, it was this possible motive and what it might be, that she was drawn to.

In any good murder investigation, finding a motive was key. Once the motive was happened upon, then a suspect could be found. Once this suspect was found, then it was just a matter of time until he was pinned to the murder. What made this case so interesting was that the suspects were already there, they just needed to be tied to a motive.

And that was what Constance was going to do. The moment that she agreed to take the case, she knew that the first thing she'd be doing would be pinning a motive to this murder. It had to be one of the workers – it had to be! All she need do was find out why one of them wanted Stu dead, and then prove they had done it. Nice and simple.

One aspect of this case that was super handy, was Mayor Brumbry's involvement. Ordinarily, Constance was forced to go behind Sheriff Nevil's back in an effort to interview witnesses. And even then, she often had to invent reasons to speak to them, never letting on that she was solving the case. It was exhausting! This time however, she was given full reign.

Mayor Brumbry called her first thing in the morning, explaining that he had spoken to Foreman Joe and the two had agreed that it would be best if she made her way out to the site in order to conduct the interviews. There, she'd have her own trailer and would be able to speak to each worker separately and at her own leisure.

It was such an ideal situation that she didn't even think to question why Foreman Joe was going along with this. She just assumed that he wanted the case over with ASAP too, and was willing to do whatever he could to make that happen.

As such, Constance arrived at the site first thing in the morning, was led to a small trailer just off from where Foreman Joe's was located, was seated at the table in the trailer and instructed to wait there until the first worker came by to answer her questions. And so, it went.

Truth be told, the whole process was rather dull and a little dragged out. There were over fifty workers that she was forced to speak to that morning, most of whom Constance was certain had nothing to do with the murder. All knew of Stu, but only a few knew him personally. And even those that knew him personally didn't count him as a friend or someone they would speak to outside of work. From what she gathered, Stu was a bit of a loner and not very well liked.

Really, she was interested in just three men, but for reasons that she couldn't comprehend, they were kept to the very end.

Tex-Mex was the first of the three, and when he saddled through the door, strutting as he made to the table, she knew she had her man. There was just something about him, a cockiness that implied he'd done the deed and was sure he would get away with it. And yes, there was some bias in Constance's assessment, but there was also some truth. She knew he was involved. He had to be!

"I hardly recognized you," Tex-Mex smirked as he took a seat opposite Constance. "If you're not on your hands and knees, scrubbing the floor, you're a different woman."

The urge to leap across the table and strangle the man was as strong as ever, but Constance refrained. "Tex-Mex, I'm glad you could make time."

"Not much of a choice, really," he snickered. "Between the foreman, and the mayor, I couldn't say no, now, could I?"

"Be that as it may, I'll keep it short."

"See that you do."

The tension between the two was palpable, and if Constance had a knife handy, she was sure she'd be able to slice right through it. Again, and now more than ever, she was certain this man had killed Stu. And what was worse, he was basically daring her to try and catch him, baiting her, dangling the lead in front of her face like the arrogant man he was... or at least that was how she saw it.

"I've looked at your report from yesterday, and you claim that you hadn't seen Stu since the previous night?"

"Not since he took that fall," Tex-Mex chuckled.

"Fell?" she queried. "You didn't push him?"

"Push him? God no!" Tex-Mex looked taken aback, even insulted by the suggestion. "Why would I go and do a thing like – he could have hurt himself!"

"And that would upset you?" she pressed with slight apprehension.

"Well how do you feel when one of your friends is hurt? Bet you don't feel like dancing." The arrogance was gone, replaced with what Constance assumed to be empathy... if that was possible?

"I didn't get the sense that you and Stu were friends."

"Oh, that." He waved her down. "We're just playing – me and all the lads are like that. But we are friends, you believe that... or at least, we were." A sniff, as if he was trying to hold back tears.

Despite herself, Constance was feeling a little confused. She had read the transcript interview between Tex-Mex and Sheriff Nevil, so she already knew what he 'claimed,' that he had nothing to do with the murder. But this was nothing like what she had expected. Not only was Tex-Mex claiming innocence, but he was claiming friendship!

"I heard you arguing with Stu, after you left the lobby," she pressed with less affirmation than she would have liked. "Any chance you could clear up what that was —"

"His birthday party," Tex-Mex said instantly. "Poor guy. We was organizing his birthday and we had a few disagreements as to what was going to be done. That's all. Perfectly innocent."

"And Piggly-Pete and Slim-Jim can confirm that?"

"They can." He wasn't smiling anymore, or smirking. Instead he appeared morose, possibly upset. Was there a chance that she had totally misread Tex-Mex? And if she had, what did that mean for the case?

"And how long have you known Stu for?" she continued, now feeling herself on the back foot.

"Years," he confirmed. "Great guy. Really, really great... yeah." Another sniff, this time with him wiping at his nose. "Do you have any idea who did this? If you need anything, ask. Don't hesitate."

"Not yet." She narrowed her eyes, trying to get a read on him. He blinked at her, looking as guilt-free as he could. "If you have any suggestions though? Did you know of any enemies he may have had?"

"I've been wracking my brain to think." He scratched at his head as if in thought. "But nah. He was pretty well loved by all. No one I can think that would want to bury him in a hole."

"I see."

When Tex-Mex left the room a few moments later, Constance was sure that he was lying. The night she had seen him with Stu, he and his friends had been rueful to the poor guy, treating him like a lesser man than they. All three of them had to be involved in some way. It was a solid premise, until she spoke to Tex-Mex. Now she didn't know what to think.

It was more of the same with Piggly-Pete and Slim-Jim too. Piggly-Pete wept openly when speaking about Stu, carrying on like the man was a brother to him. And Slim-Jim slammed his fists on the table, lamenting that he wasn't there to help protect his friend.

The two also confirmed Tex-Mex's story, that they had been arguing about his upcoming birthday party. And although this didn't make it truth, it certainly didn't help the case.

Worse too, and really the final nail in the coffin as far as Constance's suspicions went, was how supportive of each other they were. A few times, she tried to trick them into admitting that one of the other guys might have been involved, or that they might know more than they were letting on.

"That Piggly-Pete," she said to Slim-Jim, "I caught him glaring at Stu the other night. You don't know what that's about, do you?"

"Huh?" Slim-Jim rubbed at his chin. "I can't imagine what? Those two were as tight as a new pair of jeans!"

Before that, she had tried the same thing with Piggly-Pete. "Tex-Mex said that you two were arguing. Do you want to enlighten me?" she had lied.

Piggly-Pete shook his head for all it was worth, looking truly shocked; as he did, his five chins wobbled relentlessly. "I don't know. Are you sure it was me?" he responded.

That was how it was for all three of them. They were all Stu's best friends, and couldn't even begin to imagine why someone would want him dead.

Now, none of this was to say that Constance believed them... but there was really no reason that she shouldn't. They were all so darn adamant that come the end of her interview with Slim-Jim, the last of the three main suspects, she had begun to think that maybe it was time that she expanded her search. Outside of the three not-so-suspects.

"You know who I think it is?" Slim-Jim hypothesized as he leaned back in his chair.

"Who?" Constance asked with vague curiosity. She was quite sure that he wasn't about to lead her down a new path, but at this point she was willing to latch on to almost anything.

"Some of those folks from town," he said seriously." They are crazy, the lot of them. Every time I walk through town, I've never felt so hated. I guarantee, you look into them and — Oh!" He was sitting up now, reaching into his pocket and pulling out his cell.

"Who is it?" Constance asked. "Anything I should know about?"

"Na..." he mumbled as he hurriedly typed away on his phone. "I'm bidding on a new speed boat. Just got a notice that I'm still at the top... that baby is mine."

"You're bidding on a...?" Constance had no idea what the heck that meant.

"On UBuyIt," he pointed out. She looked at him dully and he confirmed, "Online."

"Oh." She nodded her head and rolled her eyes at herself. "Right, I'm just starting to get onto the whole online thing myself."

"Okay," Slim-Jim answered. There was a pause and he finished up with "Can I go, now?"

The interviews were supposed to reveal a motive. That was all. She had spoken to over fifty possible suspects, all with the intent on finding some sort of motive as to why one of them would want Stu dead. But, fifty people later – not to mention the three key suspects – and she had nothing.

By all accounts Stu was a rather boring, quiet, non-to-confrontational guy. He waved 'hello' when he walked by, he was never pushy or rude, and he kept to himself, a lot. There were only three people out of the fifty that claimed friendship with the guy, and they were the ones she'd originally assumed guilty.

If Constance wasn't so hamstrung on figuring out a way in which one of those three men might have been guilty, then she would have admitted to herself that Slim-Jim's point about the townspeople being guilty was the best lead she had. But she wasn't willing to entertain that just yet. Instead she would keep digging here. Surely, she'd find something.

"Yes, you can go," she sighed as she waved Slim-Jim away. "Just... just don't go anywhere."

"How do you mean?" he asked stupidly from the doorway.

"Never mind," she groaned as she sunk into the table, head resting in her hands.

When the sun had risen, Constance had been sure that this case would be solved come nightfall. Heck, she was sure that it would be solved come lunch. It had to have been one of the workers, and all she needed to do was speak to each one and zero in on whomever she found suspicious. What an easy day it was going to be.

Now, fifty workers later, and she had her suspicions, but nothing that was even close to concrete. Mayor Brumbry was going to be very disappointed when he found out that this case might take just a little longer to solve than she had thought. And maybe a little longer than that too.

Chapter Eight

The case was not going well at all. Constance had gone in head-strong, a little too confident, and full of zest, and had been punished as a result of it. She had interviewed all the key suspects and gotten nothing out of it. And even worse than that, not only did the key suspects give nothing away, but the interviews given seemed to further imply their innocence. They were friends with Stu, they were all best buds. None of them would have ever harmed so much as a hair on his head, let alone killed him. They were the very greatest of guys... or at least that was how they had come across.

This case was going to need some serious work. With no leads, and not much of anything really, she was in for a long night of room-pacing, hand clenching and just plain old cursing, as she tried to come up with something.

As her car approached her hotel, Constance eyed the great building with a sense of foreboding. This was the part of working a case that she had always liked the least: the grind. Now that she was about to enter into the grind, she just couldn't bring herself to do it. Therefore, it was just as she started to pull the car into the curb, that she had a quick mind change and directed the car back onto the road and into town.

A large park sat at the end of Modest Peak; connecting the small town with the mountain range that it sat just in front of, and Constance, at this exact moment, very much felt like going for a walk through it. It was just getting onto sunset by now – those interviews took all day, and that's not to mention a debrief with Mayor Brumbry afterward – and a stroll through the open space might just be what the doctor ordered. Constance's head was cluttered, and she needed to give clear it. Especially if she was going to spend the whole night re-cluttering it.

As she directed the car down the main road, she whipped her cell out and sent off a quick text to Dakota. 'Gone to park. Be back soon.' Constance would have preferred to have been at the hotel so she could keep an eye on the woman. Honestly, she had thought Sydney was bad at her job. But Dakota took it to a new level!

By the time that Constance reached the park, she decided that it was going to be a quick walk. Again, the idea of leaving Dakota alone for much longer terrified her to death. But it was as she got to walking, that she got to relaxing. The case barely even registered in her mind and as she was able to push it back and take in the moment.

Constance's life had been so go, go, go lately, with barely a pause to breathe. From moving into the house, to the engagement, through to the wedding, then the honeymoon and now the bypass. Everything around Constance was changing and it was just nice to be able to take a break and walk through a park that hadn't changed so much as a tree in the last twenty years.

It was a slow pace that Constance set for herself, one which saw her take nearly thirty minutes to reach the other side, this was despite the fact that it was barely a quarter of a mile long. The park was an open space, surrounded by dense forestry that ran right back to the mountains. By the time she reached the end, the sun was well and truly sinking below the horizon and Constance figured that perhaps it was time to be getting back.

She followed the tree line as she skirted the park, walking at a brisk pace, but not too hard. Her eyes ran over the empty park, and then through the trees, deeper into the foliage and beyond where the park started. And that was when she saw something.

It was a shadow, moving through the tree line, coming right at her. With the sun setting behind whoever it was, all she could make out was his size – much bigger than she! He grunted and groaned as he pushed through the trees. He swore and cursed as a branch slapped him in the face. But still, he kept moving.

Constance's heart skipped a beat and she quickened her pace. But she didn't run, not yet. Sense and good reason told her that it was nothing, just a hiker of some sort, coming down from the mountains.

As she hurried, she could hear the same man behind her. It sounded like he too had increased his speed, but that was unlikely. Eyes ahead, she could see her car parked some five hundred feet away. Head down, feet moving when —

From across the park, a dark figure ran straight for her. Too far away to properly make out, and hidden in the shadows cast by the trees, the dark figure made for Constance like a bull at a red flag. Now, Constance ran.

Head down, arms swinging wildly by her side, she sprinted for her car like her life depended on it... which it very much might have! Who were these men? What did they want? Surely, it had something to do with the case, but she couldn't possibly think what that might be. Especially now as she ran for her life!

As she ran, she dared a glance over her shoulder. The man in the trees had been joined now by another and as the two darkened figures broke the tree line, they turned and made for her. Three men now, all converging on Constance.

The car was two hundred feet away. She hurried. Now one hundred. She whipped her car keys from her purse as she leaped through the parking lot and ran into her car. Right into it. As she tried to go for the key hole, she tripped, fumbled, and fell into the side of her car with a thunk! Her head started to spin. She could hear the sounds of footsteps as they reached and surrounded her. It was over. Whoever this was, they had won —

"Constance? Are you okay?" Dakota yelped.

"Wha..." Constance gave her head a shake as she pushed herself up from the car. She blinked her eyes so as to readjust to the darkness, and that's when she saw Dakota, standing not five feet from her; big, curious, unblinking eyes.

"You hit the car pretty bad." Dakota floated across to Constance, taking her hand and double checking that it wasn't sprained.

"What's wrong?" Mr. Trunch, the owner of the Lone Aisle Supermarket barked as he reached the car, coming from the direction of the park.

"She fell," Dexter confirmed as he too ran toward the car, having also come from the park. "Lost her footing."

"Lucky she has footing to lose," Mr. Buck growled as he limped toward the car. His left foot was a dead club, and his knee was unable to bend as a result. This made for a slow, stunted pace.

Constance, still feeling a little confused, gave her head a shake as she hurriedly looked around the park, in search of the men that had been chasing her. There were three of them! They had been right behind her until... and that was when it dawned on her.

"It was you!" she exclaimed in anger, finger pointed dead ahead, landing on each of the men. "You three were chasing me!"

"We weren't chasing you," Dexter eased. "We just wanted to talk."

"You're the one that ran!" Mr. Trunch said matter-of-factly. "I was coming through the trees. I waved, a branch hit me in the face and you took off."

"No," Constance shook her head. She was feeling a little annoyed now at having been dismissed so off-handedly. "You were cursing. And you," she turned on Dexter. "You were coming at me like a ram on heat! What was I supposed to do?"

"My bad," Dexter grimaced as he rubbed at the back of his head. "Dakota said you'd be here and we didn't want to miss you."

"Miss me – wait. Stop everything." Constance held her hands up, as if to silence them. They all looked at her expectantly. "Why are you all here – and Dakota?! You're meant to be at the hotel." She only just realized that.

"We had to speak to you!" Dakota squeaked. "All of us!"

"About?" Constance asked desperately.

"The murder investigation," Mr. Trunch explained.

"We want to know why you are helping them!" Mr. Buck barked and spat on the ground. "Why are you against us is what we want to know."

"Against you?" Constance had no idea what the heck they were talking about. "How am I —"

"Not against us," Dakota assured her. "Just... well, we found out from Sheriff Nevil that the bypass will stop being worked on so long as this investigation is under way. And he figured that might be months!"

"Rog said that?"

"And it's not that we condone murder – no, no." The others quickly added their own 'no' each, for good measure. "But the way we see it is, if the case never gets solved, then the bypass will never start again. It's a win-win."

"So why are you helping them?" Mr. Buck snapped and spat again.

"Why not sit this one out, Constance?" Mr. Trunch asked condescendingly. "It's not good for a woman of your age to be running about like that."

"You're the one that chased me," she responded coldly.

"We just think it would be better if you left it to the police, is all." Dexter said with a big smile. "And if it never ends up getting solved then..." he trailed off, nodding his head as if he had made a point. The others agreed wholeheartedly.

And where was Constance in all of this? Confused, that's first of all. Shocked. Speechless. Unable to comprehend what was going on. Although, to be fair, she understood perfectly well what they were saying. She just couldn't believe it.

"Let me get this straight," she started slowly, making sure to catch the eyes of each individual person. "The four of you coordinated, together, to follow me out to the park, right as it was getting dark, start chasing me, and almost give me a darn heart attack?! Just so you could ask me not to interfere with a murder investigation. And all so you can keep the bypass closed for as long as possible? And this is in spite of the fact, and you really do need to know this, that at one point the bypass will be finished off. Case closed or no?" She met each person's eyes again. "Is that what you're saying here?"

"Pretty much," Dakota nodded.

"That's the long of it," Mr. Trunch agreed.

"Although to be fair, we didn't intend to give you a heart attack. Not at all," Dexter confirmed pointedly.

"Well?" Mr. Buck growled. "What will it be? Are you going to stop this or not?"

Constance didn't give him an answer. She didn't give any of them an answer... that was, except to leave. A disbelieving shake of the head was all she could give up by way of response as she turned around, opened her car door, climbed on inside, and took off.

The way that Constance saw things, the walk had produced both good news and bad news. The good news was that she no longer had to worry about the grind. She could go back to her hotel, have dinner, read a nice book and not at all feel like she was slacking. She had a break in the case, and she hadn't even been trying.

The bad news of course, was that this 'break' involved Mr. Trunch, Mr. Buck, Dakota and Dexter. The four of them were crazy people, whack jobs, capable of nearly anything as far as she was concerned. And that quite possibly, included murder.

Chapter Nine

Constance had been lying to herself before, when she had claimed that "the grind" was what she hated most about investigations. What she really hated the most, what made her skin crawl and had her hankering for a cold shower afterwards so as to wash away her sins, was investigating friends. She'd had to do it a few times over her career, and it never sat well.

There was just something inherently dirty about the concept. The idea of using her friendship to try and manipulate someone that she cared about, to try and trick them into confessing a crime, was abhorrent to say the least.

Unfortunately, there was just no way around it. Constance had been after a motive for the killing of Stu, and she had found one. A darn good one! Heck, the suspects had been the ones to give it to her. They said themselves, the murder was a good thing as it forced the bypass to shut down for the foreseeable future. They bragged about it!

If Constance had come to this possibility on her own, she probably would have dismissed it. If she were in the middle of 'the grind' and it floated into her field of view, she would have pondered it for a moment and then thrown it out as ridiculous. There was just no way that anyone she knew and associated with could kill a man all to stop a bypass from being built. It was ludicrous.

But then last night happened. That chase through the park had just about killed her, and even weirder that none of them could see what they had done wrong. They were so lost in their cause that they didn't stop to think about what they were doing.

Again, the idea of them murdering someone for this reason was the height of absurdity... but Constance couldn't be sure.

She wasn't willing to rule on the four town members just yet, but she wasn't ready to scrub them entirely. What she had to do now was some good old-fashioned police work, regardless of how slimy it felt. And if it led nowhere – which she desperately hoped – then it might at least help her make a break in the case in some sort of indirect way.

As a means to ease herself into the case, Constance decided that it would be best to start with the brother and sister coupling, Dakota and Dexter. Not only was she certain that the two were innocent, but they lived together and could thus be spoken too at the same time. Constance was all about time saving where she could.

"Constance!" Dexter beamed as he opened the front door to greet her. "What a pleasant – Dakota!" Dexter shouted over his shoulder. "You'll never guess who it —"

"Constance!" Dakota shouted from somewhere inside. "I'll be right there! Yay!"

Dexter stood in the doorway, beaming down at Constance. His brown hair was unkept and scruffy, his baby face was clean shaven and his big brown eyes didn't so much as blink once. On top of this, he was wearing a very odd-looking purple shawl that hung off his lithe body like a tent.

There was something very strange about Dexter and Dakota. And it wasn't so much that they were vegan hippies that smoked weed, used their star signs to justify weird behavior, and drank aloe vera shots like water. It was none of that. To Constance, what made them weird was that she was almost certain the two were dating, and not brother and sister at all. Although why they lied, she hadn't a clue.

But did this make them murders? She doubted it. Just weirdos.

"Constance!" As Dakota flew into the doorway, she wrapped her arms around her brother's waist and peaked her head around him. "What a lovely surprise!"

"Can I come in?" Constance asked directly. She knew these two wouldn't hesitate, so there was no need for the niceties.

"Of course!" Dakota pulled her brother from the doorway and directed her into the house. "Please, take a seat in the living room. I'll get some juice!" She turned and sprinted off into the house, leaving Constance to follow Dexter.

The house was your typical house, owned by a pair of twenty-something year-olds. Bean bags were used for chairs, posters of music artists were used for decoration, and the entire premises smelt funky. Not weird, or strange. Just... funky.

The juice that Dakota served up was orange in color, but sure as heck didn't taste like orange juice. But Constance drank it nonetheless, settling into a rather cushy bean bag chair as she did so.

"Do you like the juice?" Dakota asked eagerly. "It's made fresh from —"

"It's lovely," Constance cut her off. She really didn't feel like a laundry list of ingredients would help the flavor of the drink. She preferred ignorance. "And I'm sorry for popping in like this."

"Not at all," Dakota assured her.

"Don't be a silly billy," Dexter agreed.

"Right." Another sip of the orange colored juice. "Really, I just wanted to stop by and apologize for last night."

"Oh?" The two blinked back their surprise. "Apologize?" Dakota gasped. "What in the heavens for?"

"I was rude, in the way I left without giving the four of you an answer. Plus, I may have snapped just a touch," she grimaced as if she truly were sorry. "I shouldn't have acted that way, and I wanted to say I'm sorry."

Did Constance really feel bad about the way she had acted? And did she really think that she owed them an apology? Of course not! They'd nearly killed her in their stupidity! But she also knew that if she wanted answers, she'd have to butter them up first and lure them into a false sense of security.

It was dirty work, but it had to be done.

"And I want you to know that I am going to stop working the case too. You're right, the longer it takes to solve, the better it is for the town." She took another sip of her juice, even offering a thankful smile as she did.

"Constance!" Dakota clapped her hands together. "That's great to hear!"

"Really, just neat-o!" Dexter agreed. "We're so glad you came around. So glad!"

"Oh, I should warn you though. Sheriff Nevil will probably be stopping by later." Another sip of the juice, oh so casual.

"What? What for?" Dakota asked, the smallest hint of what may have been panic, in her voice.

"Nothing, really." Another small sip. "I just heard he's doing interviews of everyone connected to the case, gathering alibis, that sort of thing. So he can cross you off the suspect list, is all."

"Cross us off?" Dexter blinked back his shock. He looked a little put out, truth be told. "Why are we even on there?"

"Beats me," Constance shrugged. "Maybe he heard about the town hall meeting the other night, and how heated it got? I know he's working with Mayor Brumbry, so perhaps he suggested it."

"That's crazy!" Dakota cried. "We would never – we couldn't even – I'm a vegan!"

"It's fine," Constance eased, touching at her arm as a means to calm her down. "I know you two didn't do it, Sheriff Nevil too. But even still, it would be best to get your alibi in order. For the morning Stu was killed I mean. Just in case." She winked at Dakota.

"Oh, that's fine!" Dakota cried. "We have one."

"We darn sure do!" Dexter nodded his head eagerly. "And it's a good-un!"

"Oh?" Constance had to know... although something told her she wasn't going to like the answer. "What is it?"

In response, Dakota and Dexter looked at one another and smiled the most mischievous of smiles. A quick nod of the head in confirmation and the two leaped to their feet and made for the television screen across the room.

"What are you —"

"You'll see," Dakota giggled.

From behind the television, Dakota and Dexter pulled out a microphone each. They then switched the television on, changed a couple of channels and the next thing Constance knew, she was staring at some kind of karaoke set-up.

"We were competing that morning," Dexter sung into the microphone. His singing voice was a deep baritone, so unlike his speaking voice. "In Denver, from 6am until midday."

"Regional Karaoke Championships!" Dakota screamed into the microphone. She too had an excellent voice; high-pitched, yet a perfect off-set to Dexter's much deeper one. "And we wooooooooon!" Her voice boomed from the corners of the room, vibrating across the floor and up Constance's legs.

"And you, Constance Aberfield. You, get to witness history in the making as we, Captain Sparkles and Sailor Sally, perform our very own rendition —"

"A 'best in the region,' rendition," Dakota sung under Dexter's words, providing back-up.

"— version of Don't Go Breaking My Heart!" And that was exactly what they did.

For eight minutes, twice the length of the original song, Dexter and Dakota, performing as Captain Sparkles and Sailor Sally – although Constance didn't know which was which – sang and danced for Constance, while singing along to words that flashed across the screen in bright pink text.

"Don't go breaking my heaarrrtttt!" Dexter sang from one knee, eye sparkling.

"Couldn't if I tried!" Dakota cried as she reached her hand out, taking her brother's, helping him to his feet and pulling him into her.

It was perhaps the strangest moment of Constance's life, and that was regardless of the fact that the two were quite good... strange, but still good. And when Constance left their house – sprinted from it – exactly eight minutes and thirty-two seconds later, she was forced to conclude two indisputable points.

The first was that Dakota and Dexter were two very odd characters. The second was that they had an air tight alibi for the murder of Stu. Dakota and Dexter were unique, they were different, they were experimental, artsy, unusual, quirky, offbeat and a whole bunch of other things. But they weren't murderers. Constance was quite sure of that.

Chapter Ten

"9:45pm," Mr. Trunch noted as he leaned into the TV monitor, so as to double check the time-stamp in the bottom corner. "And now... no, not yet... nearly... almost there – 9:46pm."

"I believe you?" Constance moaned, trying her best not to sound rude as she did so. "You really don't have to —

"No, no," Mr. Trunch agreed. But then he frowned and touched at his chin as if in thought. "I feel like this is more accurate, less chance of being mistaken – I don't want anyone accusing me of anything funny. If you know what I mean?"

"Believe me, Mr. Trunch, no one, anywhere, will accuse you of being funny."

"Good," Mr. Trunch nodded with satisfaction. The joke, and insult, went completely over his head. Not that Constance had worried otherwise. She knew the man well, and was only too aware that humor wasn't in his wheelhouse. Mr. Trunch pointed back to the screen, right at the time stamp which now read '9:47pm.' "And if you will look here," he indicated, "The time now reads 9:47pm."

Constance stifled a groan and wiped at her eyes as a means to exaggerate her boredom. Although really, there was no need to exaggerate. Try as she might, she couldn't think of one instance where she had ever been this bored. And that was a lot to say, when considering she was currently in the middle of a darn murder investigation.

After visiting Dexter and Dakota – while at the same time trying to forget what she had been subjected to – Constance decided that Mr. Trunch, the owner of the Lone Aisle Supermarket, would be next on her list. Again, this was just a simple process of elimination as she knew Mr. Trunch quite well, and would have been rather surprised if he was a murderer. Furthermore, she knew where to find him.

Mr. Buck was going to be an entirely different matter. Although she knew where he lived, she also knew him to be a loner that would oft go hunting, or trekking, for days at a time. And even if he was home, she doubted that he'd answer the door to greet her. He was high on her list, and thus was being saved for last.

As to Mr. Trunch, Constance found him at work, seated behind his office desk as he went over the next week's schedule. Constance asked for a moment of his time, which he was only too happy to give. She then gave him the exact same spiel she had given to the Karaoke Twins, making sure to emphasize that Sheriff Nevil would be coming by later to ask for an alibi and that he best have one ready.

His word would have been enough for Constance. If he had held his hand over his heart and pledged that he had been elsewhere on the morning of Stu's murder, she would have taken that and run. But his word wasn't going to be enough. Instead, Mr. Trunch demanded – insisted! — that he show Constance his alibi... all of it.

He had been at the store that morning, from before open until after the body was found. And lucky for Constance, he just happened to have the tapes handy. As he rushed to get the tapes, Constance briefly wondered if it would have been worth running from the store, before it was too late. But she didn't, and she suffered the consequences.

For forty-five minutes Constance was forced to remain in that office, as Mr. Trunch showed her each and every single tape that featured him that morning. She was subjected to such hits as 'Mr. Trunch double checks the barcodes on each individual packet of Reese's Pieces,' and 'Mr. Trunch decides that it's time to put the older cartons of milk on sale. First at three-quarters the price, and then at half.' She watched it all, every single minute.

"Will that be enough?" Mr. Trunch asked as the last tape finished up. "Do you think that's alibi enough? I can have each of member of staff that was on that morning called up and —"

"No!" Constance was half out of her chair, hand held up as if to physically stop him from speaking, before she collected herself and relaxed. "I mean, there's no need. Save it for the Sheriff."

"Right. Right," he nodded firmly to himself as he hurried to the tape player, popped the tape out and got about labeling it. "I'll keep this close."

"You do that." Constance was already half way out the door when she started speaking, and the door was well and truly closed behind her by the time she had stopped.

It wasn't all fun and games, this police work thing. Not at all like the movies or the books made it out to be. And yet, as truly terrible as that experience was, it was as Constance hurried through the aisles of the Lone Aisle Supermarket, that there was a definite skip to her step. Mr. Trunch could be crossed off her list, well and truly. Not only was his alibi solid – so, so very solid – but after speaking to him just now, Constance was convinced that man would be incapable of killing anyone. It might not have been the most scientific analysis of a man's character, but Constance's gut told her so, and that had always been good enough for her.

And so, she was left with Mr. Buck. Of the four suspects, Mr. Buck was always the one she had suspected the most. Not only was he grumpy, angry, rude, arrogant and a lot of other superlative things in those categories, he was also strange. So very strange.

Constance had grown up in Modest Peak, and knew everyone else that had done the same – which was most of the town! And where she wasn't on speaking terms with them all, she knew them by sight. And what was more, she knew a little about each and every single one. Sometimes it was their children's favorite films, or the brand of milk that they bought. Sometimes it was where they went for holidays, or what book they were currently reading. Big or small, Constance knew a little something about everyone.

She didn't know anything about Mr. Buck. Nothing! At least not like she knew everything else. The man was about ten years older than Constance, and like she, he had spent his entire life in Modest Peak too. She had a vague idea where he lived, and she knew him to go hunting and climbing and hiking for days on end... but she didn't know where, or who with, or if that was even true!

Constance hurried through the Lone Aisle, exiting the building and taking a sharp turn toward where she thought Mr. Buck might live. Again, she wasn't totally sure, but it was a start. As she did, she nodded affirmation to herself that he was the one to follow.

His motive was as good, if not better, then the rest too. He claimed to run a small business in which he sold badges – she'd only found this out a few nights ago too – and the bypass would ruin him. He had seemed the angriest at the town hall too. All in all, it was good enough reason to give him top priority, and see what she could find out. A pleasant chat should do it, and if not... well, maybe some sleuthing would be in order.

The heavens were truly working overtime that day, for no sooner did Constance decide that it was time she spoke to Mr. Buck, that he stepped out of a store and onto the sidewalk, right in front of Constance.

"Mr. Buck!" Constance beamed her delight, absolutely smitten with how it had worked out. "Can I have a —"

"Go away!" Mr. Buck spat at Constance's feet as he hobbled away, at what must have been top pace; his right knee didn't bend, forcing him to walk with a pronounced limp.

As for Constance? She remained glued to the spot, staring at the back of Mr. Buck in total bewilderment at the way he had just acted. How rude! So much for having a pleasant chat with the man.

Chapter Eleven

The plan was a simple one: follow Mr. Buck all afternoon and see what she could find out. The execution of said plan, was just as simple.

Once Constance was able to recover from being brushed off by Mr. Buck – and rather rudely, she might add – she spun on her heel and got about tailing him. He was in the center of town, so she figured him to be doing some personal errands. And although she had no idea what she could possibly find out in this... that was sort of the idea.

As previously said, she knew next to nothing about Mr. Buck. He was a complete enigma; a total stranger that she had known her entire life. Funny that she had never thought to learn more, having seen him around town on hundreds of occasions. It had just never occurred to her that one day she'd need to know more. She needed to know more now.

One of the better things about following Mr. Buck, was that his club foot made him rather easy to tail. He didn't move very fast, and grunted and panted and puffed quite obviously wherever he went. On top of this, his gait was rather stiff – on account of the leg – so his peripheral vision was next to zero. Constance was literally able to walk right behind him, less than half a block away, and not have to worry that he would notice. Even better too that no one, anywhere, ever, would think to talk to Mr. Buck, or let him know he was being followed. It was perfect!

It was a little too perfect, as Constance was soon to find out. She had tailed perps before, and it always came with a certain excitement, and implications of danger. There was always that need to be sneaky, to hide out, remain hidden. In short, it was usually a pretty good time. Unfortunately, the complete opposite was true when it came to tailing Mr. Buck.

As Constance followed Mr. Buck from store to store, waiting just outside as he ducked in to pick up bits and bobs, she got to wondering if today could be marked as the most boring of her entire life? And yes, the incident with Dexter and Dakota made for some good storytelling, but by now it seemed a lifetime ago.

As to the stores that Mr. Buck was stopping at, none of them gave any indication as to nefarious activities. There was the butcher, the baker and yes, the candle stick maker. There was the post office and at one point, The Lone Aisle. Constance followed him into the Lone Aisle, watching with interest as he went into the back offices. At first, this got Constance's blood pumping, but then she realized they were probably just discussing the previous night, maybe setting up for another rally? She'd make sure to look into it later, but it didn't seem as relevant as it could have.

The only thing that came close to excitement was right after she followed Mr. Buck out of the Lone Aisle supermarket, only to find herself accosted by Dexter and Dakota.

"Constance!" The two called in perfect unison from across the road. "Constance! We need to talk to you!"

Constance balked as she spotted the two hurrying across the road to meet her. Worse was that Mr. Buck was walking toward them as they hurried. The three peoples crossed paths in the middle of the road and... nothing. Mr. Buck barely paid them a glance. In fact, he might have sneered.

Constance breathed for herself a sigh of relief as she kept one eye on Mr. Buck, hurrying into the DVD rental store on the opposite side of the street. Her other eye was for Dakota and Dexter, who rounded on her like a couple of bully boys.

"Is it true?!" Dakota exclaimed, throwing her hands in the air. "Tell me it isn't true!"

"Is what true?" Constance leaned around the two, making sure she could still see the entrance to the DVD store, and if Mr. Buck came out.

"That you're still working the case – say it isn't so?!" Dexter pleaded as he touched the back of his hand to his forehead. "You would never!"

"Who told you that?" she asked quickly, a little surprised they had cottoned on so quickly.

"Everyone knows," Dakota pouted. "Everyone!" she then screamed. "You told us that you had stopped. You lied!"

"Yes well..." the door to the DVD store opened and Mr. Buck hurried on out, empty handed. He took a sharp right, moving as fast as he could down the street and away from Constance. "I've got to go..." she stepped around the two and hurried across the road.

"Constance!" The two screamed in perfect unison after her. "Constance!"

"I'll speak to you tonight!" she shouted over her shoulder without turning around. "At the hotel – and get back to work!" Something told Constance that soon she'd be firing that girl, and not for murder. But that was a problem for another day.

She found Mr. Buck not five minutes later, making his way from the center of town and toward the surrounding suburbia, presumably his house. Constance kept pace as he walked to the very last street in the very end suburb, and then walked all the way to its end to literally the very last house.

Constance pulled up short, staying at the end of the street as she watched Mr. Buck enter his home. Once upon a time, it would have been a rather nice, single story, weatherboard homestead; large front yard, a balcony that skirted the entire building, and a forest sitting just behind. Yes, a very nice place... once. Now it was a bomb site. Constance wouldn't have been surprised to find that Mr. Buck hadn't once tended the lawn since his family moved in over seventy years ago.

Once Mr. Buck was inside the home, door closed up and presumably locked, Constance waited. And then she waited some more, and then a little more. She wasn't going to break into the house while he was there, but she wasn't going to just leave either. This was what police work was, waiting and watching. Something would happen eventually, and when it did, she'd be there.

Only, nothing happened. Once that door was closed, it was like he'd never gone inside. Lights off, no signs of movement. It was dead.

Constance remained about half a block down for several hours, right up until the sun had well and truly set behind the mountain range. A part of her very much wanted to wait a little longer and then break into the house when Mr. Buck was asleep... but good sense and reason told her not to. She'd come back the next day, wait until he left, and then break in. That was just common sense.

Standing in the middle of the street now, Constance chanced a final look at the house, hoping that lightning might strike twice and Mr. Buck would suddenly hurry from the front door and into the night. But not a chance. A disappointed exhale and Constance turned around only to find herself face to face with a man in a balaclava.

Her eyes popped and she opened her mouth to scream, only for the man in the balaclava to grab onto the back of her head and wrap his other hand around her mouth, effectively silencing her.

"Do not scream," the man in the balaclava whispered. His voice was deep, but a little too deep. It definitely sounded forced, probably to mask his real voice. "Understand?"

Constance nodded her head vigorously, but he didn't remove his hand. Instead he dragged her off the road, onto the sidewalk and into the shadows.

"Good." The man was taller than she, and rather skinny. She tried to look into his eyes, to see if she recognized him. But it was too dark. "Drop the case —"

"Mmmffffrrrmmm," Constance mumbled into his hand.

"Just drop it," he growled. "No more interviews. No more investigations. I've already killed once, and I will kill again if you don't stop working the case. Understand?"

Constance nodded her head as hard as she could. "Mmmmfffrrmmm," she spoke again into his hand.

"You," he spoke deeply. "If that case is solved, I'll kill you. Got it!"

For some reason, Constance didn't think so. At least not right here and now. There was something about the way he spoke and acted that made him appear non-threatening, almost like he was acting. And what was more, he didn't have a knife.

Constance didn't respond, or make to. She said nothing, waiting for her chance. The masked man frowned and asked again, "Got it?!" And still she said nothing. Nerves started to wrack him, and she could sense his confusion. He hurriedly looked over his shoulder, as if searching for someone, and that was when she lifted back her leg and kicked him square in the shin.

"Owww!" he screamed. Really, it was more of a wail. His deep voice broke as he threw back his head and cried into the night. And Constance took her chance.

She gave him a hard shove, throwing him off her as he tripped up and struggled to regain his balance. Constance used that time to quickly kick off her slip-on flats, turn on her heel and run for all she was worth.

Oh, how she sprinted. Chest puffed out, knees coming up nice and high, short and sharp arm movements with deep, controlled breathing. She had done a lot of sprinting since taking up detective work, and after a while you just started to learn how.

And as she ran, she listened behind for the sound of the man in the balaclava following her. If her luck held, he would give up, convince himself she had gotten the message and go home. She did get the message, but probably not the one he wanted.

In the process of her investigation, Constance had successfully rattled someone's cage. The question now was, who's had she rattled? But that was a question to be answered later. Right now, she had to run.

Chapter Twelve

The attack on Constance hadn't upset her anywhere near as much as it should have. Someone had molested her in the middle of the street, threatened her life, and then forced her to leave a pair of her favorite shoes behind in the process so that just anyone could come along and find them. She should have been shaking from the experience!

But really, she was fine. The sprint had done much to calm her down, and the more she thought about it, the more she decided that whoever had attacked her wasn't an actual threat. Yes, they had threatened her, but indirectly. They wanted her off the case and claimed that they would do anything it took to make it happen.

"The whole thing is rather redundant, don't you think?" she asked Sheriff Nevil casually from the chair in the interrogation room.

"Redundant? Redundant?!" Sheriff Nevil exclaimed, pulling at his hair as he paced the room. "Someone threatened your life, Constance! I don't see how that's —"

"They threatened my life, but only if I don't stop looking into this murder. But they didn't stop to think that murdering me would only incriminate them further. Very silly, don't you think?"

The look Sheriff Nevil gave Constance could only be described as 'what on God's green earth are you talking about?' Expression aghast, hair sticking up on all ends, and mustache an absolute mess, Sheriff Nevil wasn't taking this situation nearly as calmly as Constance.

Already, Constance was regretting having run to the police station. Oh yes, she ran. It was an eight-minute walk from where she had been to the police station, but running, Constance did it in just over two minutes. She did consider just going straight home, but knew this was probably the type of thing she needed to report. And so, she did, and here she was... regretting it.

"This is serious, Constance!" Sheriff Nevil exclaimed. "One body, with the threat of a second! It's nowhere near the small thing you seem to think it is."

"Maybe I've just had more time to process it," she said off-handedly.

"Let's run through this." He was speaking to himself more than Constance. Still pacing the room, he ticked each point off on a finger. "We have Stu, found dead and buried. I start investigating the case immediately, and nothing. Not a peep from nobody. You then come into the case, speak to the same people and next thing —"

"Correction." She sat up and held a finger in the air. "I spoke to Dexter, Dakota and Mr. Trunch too. Remember?"

"Yes, yes," he dismissed, waving her down as he continued to pace. "But they're not responsible for the death of Stu..." Sheriff Nevil paused, turned to face Constance and waited for her agreement."

"I don't think so," she shook her head.

"Good." He started pacing again. "Therefore, it stands to reason that whoever attacked you is from the site. One of those guys got nervous after you started asking questions, and figured he'd put a stop to it before you got any closer – and I know the point you just made. But remember, these guys aren't known for their smarts."

"Can I interject for a moment?" Constance pushed herself to stand. "It is my case, after all —"

"You're case?!"

"Being attacked, I meant." She smiled innocently and blinked. "Not the ah... you know..."

"Oh, the murder?" He put his hands on his hips as if to shame her. "The one you promised you wouldn't get involved with? The one that you looked me in the eyes and said—"

"It was Mayor Brumbry!" she snapped. They had already been over this; with him scolding her, her apologizing and explaining, and then him forgiving her. "You try saying no to him – and that's not the point!"

"What is?"

"I think I know who attacked me."

This received the appropriate amount of shock from Sheriff Nevil. Struck speechless, his mouth kind of just opened and closed like a goldfish.

"You always had a way with words," she smirked before carrying on. "Look, I don't think the person that attacked me just now killed Stu. My gut says that he just didn't have it in him."

"Oh, your gut said that?" he responded dryly.

Constance's nostril's flared at Sheriff Nevil before continuing. "And more to that point, like I said, I think I know who it was. In fact, I'm sure of it."

That run to the police station may have been short, but it provided plenty of time for Constance to run over what had just happened in her head, break it down, and then come up with an answer.

First were the attacker's demands. He seemed more interested in her dropping out of the case, rather than making sure the case wasn't solved at all. He could have demanded that she bungle the evidence, or lead them down the wrong path. But no, it was plain and simple. Whoever this was, wanted the case to drag out for longer than it would if she was on it.

Second was the voice. That deep, fake baritone was surprisingly smooth. And when paired with that glass shattering howl, that was perfectly on pitch, there was really only one person it could be.

"Dexter attacked me," she sighed as she slumped back into her chair. "It had to be him."

"Dexter? The kid that works for Jonas?"

Constance nodded her head. "He and his sister weren't very happy to hear that I was working the case. They seemed to think that mine doing so ensured that it would be solved." She offered a satisfied smirk at the Sheriff, before continuing. "And seeing that they want this bypass done away with, the figured this was the way to go about it."

"Well... are you sure?" All the energy had left Sheriff Nevil, now that he was starting to agree with her.

"Pretty sure," she nodded as she thought. She couldn't make him out exact, but the rest was too much of a coincidence for it not to be the case. "I was right that they were whackjobs – his sister too, and the others. Not killers... but not stable either."

"What do you want to do?" Sheriff Nevil leaned against the wall, his arms folded.

"Not press charges, obviously. I think that I'll be stopping by their house on the way home though, letting them know that next time they attack me, they better be packing."

Sheriff Nevil chuckled and pushed himself back up. "I'll come. It might have more effect if the Big Boss is with you. Scare the law back into them."

"All right, but if they start singing karaoke, I'm out."

"Huh?"

***

"I really don't know where this is coming from!" Dakota was all blubber and tears; they fell thick and heavy down her cheeks, smudging her make-up, running down her neck and wetting the top of her shirt.

"I just told you where," Constance said as she reached across and tried to take Dakota's hand. Dakota wasn't having any of it though, pulling her hand back as if she had been bitten by a snake. "It's not personal."

"It sure feels that way! And after we sung for you!"

"It's okay, Dakota." Dexter sat right by Dakota; his arm wrapped around her shoulder in a loving, caring embrace. Unlike his sister, he wasn't crying, or even that upset looking, to be honest. "They're just doing their job."

"Well it's a stupid, silly, dumb dumb job!" Dakota cried. Mucus was now coming from her nose, blowing itself into a large bubble before suddenly bursting. Dexter wiped at it for his sister, and then wiped it off on his jeans.

Constance was seated on the same beanbag chair as earlier, while she watched the little performance with about as much patience as she could muster – she was the one who had been attacked! And yet it was Dakota who was carrying on. This was even more strange as it was Dexter that she and Sheriff Nevil had come here to accuse, yet it was Dakota acting like she was in the firing line.

Sheriff Nevil stood by Constance, choosing not to sit. She dared a glance at him – in between the nose blowing – and was surprised at how put-out he looked. She would have assumed that this kind of thing was common place. Apparently not.

"Dakota, if you could just... take it easy for a moment?" Constance tried. Again, she leaned forward to take Dakota's hand and again Dakota snatched it away.

"Why should we?" she blasted. "You come in here... accuse my brother of attacking you! And... and... and it's just so unfair!" She threw her head back and wailed.

There were two options here, as far as Constance could tell. The first was to shrink back and try and salvage the situation. She could have apologized, said she had gotten it wrong, and moved on. From there it would have been a process to follow Dexter and catch him in the act again. This was not an option.

The second option, and the far more likely, was to snap Dakota out of her funk the only way Constance knew how.

"That's enough!" Constance roared, suddenly pushing herself to her feet. "These crocodile tears might work on other people, but not on me. Understand?!"

The effect was instantaneous. Dakota stopped crying. The brother and sister pair seized up, clutched onto one another and leaned back as Constance towered over them. They blinked. They gawked. But they didn't speak. They were far too shocked for that.

Even Sheriff Nevil was taken slightly aback. He leaned forward and touched Constance on the shoulder. "Constance... do you think you might want to take it easy —"

"No, Rog, I don't." She didn't turn back to look at him, choosing to keep her stare firmly on Dakota and Dexter. "We've been nothing but fair with these two, and if they think they can cry their way out of this like a couple of five-year olds, then they have another think coming. It's time to face the music and admit to what you have done. So... come on now... admit it!" She looked from Dakota to Dexter, pausing on each for a moment, waiting for one of them to break. One of them had to break.

This wasn't an official interrogation, or anything even close to it. Constance knew Dakota well, and knew Dexter well enough. She knew that neither had meant her harm and that their little 'attack' was an error in judgment and nothing more. Where Sheriff Nevil had suggested pressing charges, she had shot him down. 'Scaring some sense into them,' would do the trick, she thought.

But as Constance beared down on the two, trying her best to scare some sense into them, she could tell almost immediately that it wasn't going to work. Dakota had seemed genuinely upset that Constance had accused Dexter of such a thing, and

Dexter had seemed utterly perplexed. Was there a chance that he wasn't the man who had attacked her?

"There's nothing to admit," Dexter said firmly, chin pointed higher... although it did wobble just a tad. "I've been here all night – Dakota too. We were —"

"We were practicing!" Dakota pleaded. "You've seen us perform. You know what's at stake here for us – with Nationals coming up! We can't afford not to practice every second we get."

"She's right," Dexter nodded. "We've been at it for the last three hours at least."

"Do you have any proof?" Sheriff Nevil sighed from behind Constance. "Other than your good word?"

The two shook their heads. "Isn't our word enough?"

Once upon a time, it just might have been. But these were strange times and as much as Constance hated to admit it, Dexter and Dakota were very quickly making their way up the list of suspects. Now, did she think that these two had anything to do with the murder of Stu? And did she think that the attack from earlier was linked to it in any way either? Honestly, no she didn't. But she had been wrong before.

"We're going to leave now," Constance said slowly, carefully, as if she was speaking to a skittish cat. "And as to this whole... whatever it was. We're going to pretend it never happened. How's that sound?"

The two nodded their heads eagerly. Dakota even managed to stop crying, sniffing and wiping away the tears from her eyes as she did.

"Good," Constance said.

"Constance?" Sheriff Nevil started. "Are you sure you want to —"

"I am." She kept her eyes trained on the two. They were shaking now; the adrenaline leaving their bodies. "They said they didn't do it, so I believe them. I just hope, I really, really, really hope, that it doesn't happen again." A final glare followed by a smile. "Let's go."

"Okay," Sheriff Nevil agreed. He shared a final look for Dakota and Dexter. "Just know that I'm watching —"

It sounded like a police siren, wailing from just outside the house. But another second and Constance realized it to be a car alarm. It rang out; loud and obnoxious, calling for all in the area to come and see.

"Whose car is that?" Sheriff Nevil shouted as she strode to the front door. "It's not – God darn it!" He threw the door open and charged outside.

Constance was right behind him, hurrying from the house and outside, into the night, to where the noise was coming from. She didn't have to run far though. No sooner was she out of the house, did she see the source of the car alarm. Really, it was hard to miss.

It was Sheriff Nevil's police car. Someone had taken a bat or club to it, smashing the front and back windows, and denting the doors. But that wasn't what had Constance gaping. What she couldn't take her eyes off was the red spray painted message, scrawled across the side door. 'Close. But way off!'

"No, no, no, no, no," Sheriff Nevil cried as he gently touched at the car, as if worried the whole thing would fall apart. "No, no, no!" He shook his hands in the air.

Still reeling from the shock, Constance pulled her eyes from the car, from that message, and turned back toward the house. Dakota and Dexter stood in the doorway, both looking about as surprised as she felt. Dexter had claimed that he wasn't the one who attacked her a few hours previously and now, despite her previous assumption, she was forced to admit that he might have been telling the truth.

Chapter Thirteen

"Close. But way off?" Mayor Brumbry repeated each word slowly, with extra emphasis, as if he had never heard any of the words spoken out loud before; as if it were an alien language that he was only just starting to wrap his head around.

"That's what it said." Constance nodded her head as she stifled a yawn and took a seat at the dining room table. Breakfast was already served up in front of her – bacon and eggs, courtesy of Jonas – and she had been hoping to get stuck into it before she started her day. No such luck.

It was early in the morning, far too early for this conversation. When Constance had heard someone banging away on her door, she had assumed it would be Sheriff Nevil. Since the previous night, he had resigned himself to the fact that Constance was now on the case, and appeared only too happy work it with her. It was a small thing, but in Constance's mind it was a blessing as it would really make the whole process that much earlier. She knew that he would eventually come around, and this just saved the arguing process.

Despite this sudden approval from the sheriff, it was still much too early, and as Constance went to open the front door, she was all but ready to give him a wicked tongue lashing, one that would have him licking his chops for a few hours. What was he thinking, coming to her house this early? Someone had better be dead! But when Constance opened the door, she saw that it wasn't Sheriff Nevil standing on her front porch. It was Mayor Brumbry.

The shock of seeing the mayor hammering on her door so early in the morning was such that

Constance barely had time to react before the mayor pushed her aside, barged into her home and then started carrying on about the case and how he needed it done with. Now!

"I heard you had a solid lead," he carried on as he made his way through the house and toward the kitchen. "Something to do with those whackadoodles at the town hall meet – is that bacon?!" He pointed eagerly at a tray of freshly cooked bacon on the kitchen counter.

With no real choice, Constance served the mayor up a plate of bacon. And then, the two got about eating it – with the mayor helping himself to some freshly squeezed juice – as she got about explaining everything that had happened so far.

When she finished with the story, culminating at the previous night with the vandalism of Sheriff Nevil's car, the mayor looked appropriately confused. He chewed on the end of a piece of bacon, his eyes narrowing as his thoughts aligned.

"Close. But way off," he spoke again, this time sounding more sure of himself.

"That's what it said," Constance sighed. She had been looking forward to eating a very large breakfast, but ended up settling for about half. "I figure it was from whoever attacked me. Playing with me. But why they saw the need now? I haven't had time to puzzle that out just—"

"Isn't it obvious." Bacon bits flew from Mayor Brumbry's mouth. "It's as clear as day!"

"Okay?" Constance suppressed a groan. She knew where he was going with this, but hoped she was wrong.

"It was him! It had to be him – the same person who attacked you! And who killed Stu too. He attacked you in the park to warn you off, and then he sprayed the car to... I don't... to get in your head. Yes, that's it. It's all linked!"

She knew he'd say that. "I don't think so."

"How come?" he demanded.

"Well... it doesn't make any sense for one." Mayor Brumbry opened his mouth to argue, so she raised her voice and spoke over him. "If it was the man who attacked me, then why give himself up like that? If he saw that I was investigating someone else, why would he correct my course? If anything, he should want me to set my sights on Dexter, not turn away. And besides, why would he warn me to stay away from the case, and then bait me to keep investigating it?" It was mixed messaging at its best, and it was doing Constance's head in.

"So what then? The person who attacked you isn't the murderer? They're not linked at all? Is that what you think? How can that be?!" The mayor was getting flustered now, his round face turning red, his eyes blinking furiously.

Constance had no idea what any of it meant. She had tried to break it down several times already, but had failed at every turn. What she had been hoping for was a nice big breakfast to clear her head and give her something to work with... but that wasn't going to happen either.

The person who graffitied Sheriff Nevil's car must have been the same person who attacked her on the street. For whatever reason, he had seen her go to Dexter and Dakota's house and decided to warn her off that lead... but why he would do that, she didn't have a clue. And then there was the bigger question of 'how did this fit in with the murder of Stu?' If at all? Whoever murdered Stu obviously didn't want her working the case... but apparently also didn't want her working the wrong angle of the case.

It was enough to make Constance's head spin. What she really wanted to do was go back and speak to those construction workers again. She had gotten herself on a bit of a tangent in following the townspeople, a tangent which she sensed was leading her nowhere. Something just told her that she had been a little too quick to dismiss the construction workers, and another thorough investigation of them was in order.

But it was as she started to settle on this very obvious and practical idea, that she took note of Mayor Brumbry suddenly sitting up, his eyes growing in size while a satisfied smile took over his face.

"I've got it!" He was on his feet now, finger pointed in the air, looking positively delighted in himself. "By Joe, I have it!" Then, calming down, he smiled broadly at Constance, nodding his head to himself in satisfaction. "You know, this whole detecting thing really isn't that hard, if you ask me."

Constance suppressed a sigh. "Okay. Tell me."

"The townspeople." He couldn't have sounded more sure of himself. "They're working together! They have to be working together!"

"I don't think so," Constance said calmly. "I just don't see them as killing anyone. Honestly, I want to go back to the bypass and speak to the workers again —"

"Think about it," Mayor Brumbry cut her off as he started pacing the room, wringing his hands together excitedly. "They knew you were on to them, after those interviews you did. So, to scare you off, one of them came after you – Jackson?"

"Dexter," she corrected.

"Right, Dexter. He came after you, knowing that you would suspect it was him. And then, when you went to his house, one of the other ones came out and sprayed the police car. That way you'd have no choice but to stop looking into him! It's perfect!"

It wasn't half bad, and Constance was big enough to admit it. The only real spanner in the works was that she didn't suspect them to be killers. But then again, there was also the chance that the two cases were separate. That was something she was yet to truly consider.

"It makes sense," she admitted. "But —"

"No buts." Mayor Brumbry had stopped pacing now, instead turning on Constance and baring down on her like he was her boss, scolding her for doing the job wrong. "I brought you onto this case Ms. Aberfield, because I was told that you were the kind of detective that thought outside the box."

"I am," she said through a clenched jaw. It was a condescending remark, and one she didn't much appreciate.

"Well! Think outside the box will you! I know you have an attachment to these people, but they are clearly unhinged! And they need to be stopped before they do anymore damage."

"Even if it was true. We don't have any actual evidence."

"Then get some!" he threw his hands in the air. "What about that hermit – Mr. Buck? You said that you haven't spoken to him yet."

"I have not."

"So you haven't been to his house either?"

"No."

"That's it then!" He started nodding to himself, eyes dancing. "What if... Okay, here is what we're going to do."

"We?" Constance bit her tongue to stop herself from saying something she would regret. Mayor Brumbry had just inserted himself right into her case, and no, she was not very happy about it.

"Yes, yes, we. I'm going to call up this Mr. Buck, have him meet me. Tell him that I want to speak about this bypass. And then, when he's out of the house, you can break in and have a little look. See if you can't find something? How does that sound?"

It sounded unethical, is how it sounded. But worse than that, it sounded just like something that Constance would have done, had she been so inclined. The only thing stopping her from getting excited about the plan was that she didn't think Mr. Buck was guilty... and that she hadn't come up with the idea either.

Unfortunately, Mayor Brumbry was proving a very hard character to say no to. He was still on his feet, looking down at Constance with the look of a man that would have to be physically wrestled from the house before admitting defeat. And even though Constance was pretty sure she could take him, if it came to that, she wasn't about to tackle the mayor.

"Fine," she sighed, throwing her hands up and admitting defeat. "Tell me what I have to do."

In a way, this was a good thing... at least Constance told herself that. The more she thought about it, the more she decided that the townspeople just weren't responsible for the murder of Stu. But the only way to be sure was to upturn every last stone. Once this little mission was done with, she'd be able to turn her attention back to the construction workers and finally get about solving a murder. That was why she was hired, after all.

***

It was with great reluctance that Constance found herself sneaking into Mr. Buck's home less than an hour after her impromptu-breakfast with Mayor Brumbry. As a means to make herself feel better about the act, she told herself that it was just a means to an end. She'd have a sneaky look through his things, find nothing concrete to pin on him, and then be done with this loose thread.

Unfortunately, this plan could only happen if Constance went inside the hermit's house, and that was not something she was relishing in doing. When she had seen the house the previous day, she had remarked that it looked as if it had never once been tended too. The moment she snuck through the back yard and stepped onto the back deck, she was sure this to be the case.

The entire place was just filthy. Even 'filthy' didn't really do the house justice in terms of how grotesque it was. The backyard was overgrown. The wood being used to make up the balcony was covered in slime and ash from cigarettes. Even the window, which she had to pry open as a means to fall into the house, was sticky and left a very peculiar smell on her fingers.

The inside was no better. Mr. Buck clearly had a problem with throwing things away... anything at all. Among the piles of clothes, stacks of furniture, and towers of books, CDs, and everything else he had ever bought in his life, were dozens and dozens of full garbage bags. Constance wanted to hurl, and that had nothing to do with the smell.

She made her way through the house, wondering what on earth she could possibly find. Even if she did find something, it would have been nearly impossible to detect. There was just so much junk in the house that she could have very well stepped over a dead body and not even noticed.

And yet, the moment that Constance did find some evidence, she knew it right away. It was like a sixth sense, drawing her toward it, calling to her from the other room. She could feel the pull as she stepped through the living room and into the bedroom.

The evidence in question was a fluro-yellow workman's vest, much like the one that the construction workers wore all day while on site. It was lain out on the bed, as if on display. More than that, a closer look and Constance could see the logo for the crew that she knew to be in charge of the bypass. This belonged to one of the workers... or at least it had.

Constance groaned as she fell down to her knees so as to get closer to the vest. A vest didn't mean anything. She knew that Mr. Buck liked to go for hikes, and the chances were that he had just found this on one of his walks. That was the most likely explanation. But then she looked a little closer.

Lining the hem of the vest, on the right-hand side, was what could only be a blood stain. She then picked the vest up, looked inside the lining and found the name 'Stu' scrawled in black ink.

"Well, dang," she said to herself as she eyed the blood and signature. "I guess I was wrong." She would never say those words out loud for anyone to hear. But she was alone, so she felt it was okay.

But the takeaway here was that Constance had been wrong. Mr. Buck, it seemed, had killed Stu. What an odd, and unexpected turn.

Chapter Fourteen

The case was a wrap. Done and dusted. Ground to an end. Well and truly solved.

Once Constance found the blood-stained vest, she got herself out of that house and gave the mayor a call. He was over the moon with her discovery, promising that it would be she that got the bulk of the plaudits.

"No, no, Ms. Aberfield," he assured her over the phone. "It was all you. I was merely a vessel in which you channeled your brilliance!"

"Thanks?" It felt like the right thing to say, even though it didn't sit right. For some reason, Constance wasn't feeling how she usually did after solving a case. Ordinarily she was abuzz with energy, brimming with self-confidence, absolutely bursting at the seams at a job well done. But not this time.

"I'll meet you at the station," the mayor finished. "No need to call the Sheriff, I already have."

"What? How have you —"

"I mean that I will!" The mayor interrupted. "Sorry, I'm just a little excited is all." She could practically see him dancing on the other end of the line.

Constance rolled her eyes, said goodbye, and then did as he instructed and made her way to the police station. From there she was fully expecting a long, arduous process. There were going to be more interrogations, cross interrogations, witness reports and paperwork. She was then going to have to explain what she was doing in Mr. Bucks house in the first place and hope that Sheriff Nevil could help bypass the law just enough so as not to dismiss the evidence.

And that wasn't to mention the stern talking to he was going to give her. It was going to be a long day. At least that was what Constance had assumed right up until the moment she arrived.

Constance didn't know who Mayor Brumbry had spoken too, once he was off the phone with her, but it must have been someone important. No sooner had Constance arrived at the police station was she being told that a search warrant had already been green-lit and soon they'd have the blood-stained vest in their possession. All totally legal.

"But how?" Constance asked with confusion as Sheriff Nevil quickly explained the situation to her. "That doesn't make any —"

"Mayor Brumbry made some calls, I guess." Sheriff Nevil shrugged. "Hey, who cares how? We got him." He gave Constance's arm a quick pat as if to assure her she had done the right thing; this was despite the fact that even he didn't sound so sure.

But Constance, and she guessed Sheriff Nevil too, could sleep tight knowing that in the end, the right thing would be done. So what if she had skirted the law slightly? If a murderer was captured, then the ends justified the means. If the blood came back as a match for Stu, then Mr. Buck was certainly guilty. The end result was what mattered here. It was a fair conclusion to make... so why was there still a nagging feeling deep in Constance's self-conscious.

This pestering feeling followed her the entire day. It sat right beside her as she remained at the police station, waiting for Sheriff Nevil to come back. And it seemed to rest squarely on her shoulders as he explained to her later in the day that the blood did indeed match that of Stu's. And when it came to the actual interrogation of Mr. Buck, the pestering feeling seemed to have found its way inside of her, squirming and moving around her stomach, making her feel ill.

"I didn't do nothing!" Mr. Buck protested, punching at the interrogation table, which he was also handcuffed too.

"Tell that to the blood-stained vest we found in your apartment," Sheriff Nevil responded coolly. He was leaning back in his chair, smirking his delight at Mr. Buck. It was all part of his interrogation technique, designed to break the man down. "Blood that matches the victim. Oh, and did we mention that the victim's name was on the vest too?"

"I don't know nothing about that!"

Constance was watching the whole thing from behind the double-sided mirror in the adjacent room. She stood with a few other officers, and Mayor Brumbry himself. The mayor had been smiling and carrying on all day, not even trying to hide how happy he was. Indeed, as he watched Sheriff Nevil try and break Mr. Buck, he wrung his hands together like a starving man staring at a freshly baked turkey, beaming his delight

"I spoke to the Sheriff earlier too," the mayor said to Constance. He never once took his eyes off Mr. Buck. "The site will be opening back up first thing tomorrow. Isn't that just wonderful?!"

"Wonderful," she muttered to herself.

"Look, Mr. Buck, if you tell us the truth, this will go a lot easier on you." Sheriff Nevil unfolded his arms and leaned forward on the table. His voice was softer now, his eyes pleading. "I want to help."

"I am telling the truth!" Mr. Buck barked. "I didn't kill no-one."

"Where were you the morning that Stu was killed?"

"Home, sleeping. Is that a crime now? Huh?"

Sheriff Nevil pushed himself back and re-crossed his arms. "And I suppose that you didn't vandalize my car either?"

"I don't know anything about that..." He shifted in his seat, his eyes suddenly looking everywhere but at Sheriff Nevil.

Constance was against the glass now, face pressed right into it. Up until this point in the interview, she had felt bad for Mr. Buck. She had dealt with a lot of liars in her time, and she was certain that he wasn't lying... either that or he was a magnificent liar. But his response to the vandalism accusation was what had her in a state.

Mr. Buck was adamant that he was innocent in the murder of Stu. He swore it! And it sounded like the truth. But his denial of vandalizing Sheriff Nevil's car was nowhere near as earnest. It almost sounded to Constance like he had done it, but was denying it simply because he thought he should.

"That's... weird..." Constance said to herself.

"What?" Mayor Brumbry half-asked. He was still staring at Stu as if worried the man might make a break for it.

"The car. Why did that question have him change his demeanor so much? Weird that a petty vandalism charge would affect him so."

"What do you mean? I just heard him deny the charge." The mayor was still watching Stu, but his interest had now shifted to Constance.

"Yeah... but not in the same... never mind." She bit her lip in thought.

Something wasn't right. And it wasn't just the arrest of Mr. Buck that felt off, but everything before that. Constance had a sixth sense like a cat, and she knew better than to ignore it. And so, as Mr. Buck continued to pleaded his innocence, and as Mayor Brumbry watched the show like it were a baked ham, she delved back into her minds-eye, desperate to figure out what was bothering her.

When the body of Stu had first been found, she had been certain that one of the workers was responsible. They were the only people in town that had any connection to him, and thus the only ones that had any reason to kill him. But when she got to speaking to them, their stories all put them in the clear. And then some! They couldn't have been more innocent by the way they told it.

It was because of this unwavering support of one another that she turned to the townspeople. They had a motive, and they had proven themselves to be a little unhinged when it came to stopping this bypass. So why not? But the more she looked into them, the less likely it seemed. Yes, they were a little nuts, but not killers.

And then there was the random attacker. She would have sworn black and blue it was Dexter, trying to put the fear in her to drop the case. But when the police car was vandalized while he was in the house – presumably by the same person that attacked her – it scrubbed him from the list of suspects.

Common sense told Constance that the murder, the attack, and the vandalism were all done by the same person. And yet whenever Constance tried to settle on this as fact, she just didn't feel right. And yes, Mr. Buck did have that vest in his house. But even that was strange in the way it had happened. It was almost like he, or the killer at least, had known Constance would be going there at one point and lain it out for her. But how? And why?

There was more to this case then Constance had managed to uncover, and she had to find out what.

"I've got to go," she said quickly as she turned and made for the door.

"Where are you going?" Mayor Brumbry called after her. He didn't make to stop her, or even bother looking up.

"For a walk. Clear my head. That kind of thing." She popped the door open and went to step out.

"Okay," Mayor Brumbry called out vaguely. "I'll call you when he breaks."

Constance didn't respond, shutting the door behind her before he even finished speaking. Mr. Buck wasn't going to break, and that was because he didn't do it. Whoever the killer was, whoever had attacked Constance, whoever had vandalized Sheriff Nevil's car, and whoever had planted that vest in Mr. Buck's house, was still out there somewhere, and Constance was going to find out where.

Chapter Fifteen

At nighttime, with no traffic to contend with, it was less than a fifteen-minute drive from Modest Peak to where the bypass started, to where the body of Stu had been found. Fifteen minutes of silence. Fifteen minutes without Mayor Brumbry or Sheriff Nevil whispering in her ear. Fifteen minutes for Constance to go over the case, step by step, without having to worry about being interrupted.

It was a fifteen-minute drive to the site, and Constance intended – and did – use every single one of them.

The site was empty when she arrived, with the few sources of light coming from inside the assorted trailers, peeking out from behind the closed blinds. These were the workers the hadn't managed to secure a spot in her hotel, the ones that slept here at night, and then worked come morning. In order to avoid being seen or heard, Constance made sure to park her car a little ways down the road and out of sight.

When the car was safely hidden, she hurried back toward the site, following the newly constructed road as she made for where Stu's body had been found. She did a double check of her pockets too, making sure she had her cell phone handy. It was a moonless night and she could scarcely see a thing, so the last thing she needed was to trip over and break her own neck. Wouldn't that cause a fuss!

Bent over so as not to be seen, and scurrying along the road like a mouse in the night, Constance had finally managed to settle on the two main points that had been eating away at her since she had woken up; two points that really had her questioning whether Mr. Buck had killed Stu.

The first point was this: Why Stu? If it was Mr. Buck that had done the killing, why had he chosen Stu of all people to kill. The man had no connection to him as far as she knew. Was he a random choice? Was he the first-person Mr. Buck had come across? There were over fifty people working the site, so the fact that Stu was the one that ended up dead was puzzling.

The second was the actual location of the body. The motive to stop the bypass from happening by killing a random worker was a solid one to be sure, but the location that the body was found in completely undercut this plan. If it wasn't for Constance and her trip down memory lane, then the body may not have been found for weeks, or even months! If they had truly killed Stu as a means to stop the bypass, then they would have dumped the body right where everyone could see it.

It was these two points that had Constance concluding very matter-of-factly that something wasn't right about this case. Now, it was up to Constance to find out what... and if she was lucky, why.

Getting to the location where Stu's body was found proved harder than Constance had originally anticipated. First of all, the entire forest was fenced off. There was a six-foot high wire fence built around the perimeter as a means to keep out intruders, and Constance. As such, she was forced to climb up the side of the wire fence like a cat in the night; throwing her leg over and then tumbling to the other side and into the dirt... very un-cat like. The whole thing would have been funny had it not hurt so much.

From there, it was a matter of picking her way through the forest, in the pitch blackness of the night, and hoping she didn't get lost. And sure, she had a phone with a light, but it only did so much. There were a lot of branches to duck under, stumps to climb, bushes to push past and random shadows that she skirted rather than going through. And that wasn't to mention the noise!

Oh, the sounds that Constance had to ignore; for her sanity if nothing else. Coming from every direction were the snarls of wild beasts, the cries of harpies, the calls of muggers, rapists and murderers. With every step she took, these sounds only got closer and closer and closer until they were nearly right upon her. She tried to remind herself that it was unlikely that any of these sounds were what she imagined, and that her mind was just playing tricks. But gosh darn, it was hard.

By the time that Constance had breached the clearing, stumbling into the quarry and nearly down into the empty basin, she was just glad to be alive. But then she straightened herself up, took a deep breath and realized that all those sounds that were following her had stopped dead... almost as if they were never there at all.

Chuckling to herself, and giving her head a shake, Constance redirected her attention to the center of the basin. In order to get there, she had to climb down the side of the rockface – again, a task that was easier in the light – and then step around the yellow tape that cut off the exact location of the body.

And then, finally, Constance was there.

There was nothing particularly interesting about the site. It was an open space, covered in rock and dirt... and that was about it. The spot where Stu's body had been found had since been dug up, with the dirt piled beside the hole, but all actual evidence was gone.

And besides, there was never that much actual evidence in the first place. That was the main reason that Constance hadn't yet returned to the scene of the crime. From what she had been told, and read, Stu was killed off site, via stabbing, and then dumped here, buried deep in the ground. They had no idea where he was killed, or how his body had arrived at the site.

Constance had her hands on her hips as she walked the edges of the basin, looking up the rock face and back into the forest. Something wasn't right here. Again, she was forced to ponder on her realization that whoever dumped his body out here didn't want it to be found. But there was more.

This was one darn hard place to get to, especially if you had a body to carry. There was no way that a single person could carry a body here unseen. And then there was the matter of digging up the dirt to make a whole big enough to bury Stu, dumping him in that hole, and then covering him back up. That would take manpower! And if not manpower, then a machine of some sort, one that someone like Stu certainly didn't have access to.

Constance hurried back to the hole in the ground. She bent down on both her knees and pawed at the dirt, even going so far as to dig it up with her fingers. It was hard packed and tough to dig through. The person who dug this whole was either very experienced in hole digging, had some sort of machinery to make it easier... or there was more than one —

"What the hell are you doing?!" Sheriff Nevil shouted from behind Constance, sending her jumping about ten feet in the air. And that wasn't to mention the way that her heart leapt through her throat, out her mouth and ran off into the forest so as to hide.

"Rog!" Constance gasped as she spun around and clutched at her chest. "What are you... what... you scared me!" She managed through deep breaths. Her heart was racing and her blood was pumping. Oh, she could kill him!

It Sheriff Nevil, standing not ten feet away in the darkness. At least he had been standing, once. Now, he was bent over, slapping at his thighs and clutching his sides in amusement. "I need to get me one of those whaddya call it – GoCams. Strap it to me head and record this stuff! Jesus you jumped so high that —"

"While you're at it, you can record my foot disappearing up your butt too. Jesus, Rog! What's the matter with you – and what are you doing here!" Fear had been over taken by anger at this point, and Constance wasn't afraid to show it.

Sheriff Nevil sobered himself up as he crossed the rest of the quarry to meet Constance in the middle. He was alone, and had with himself a flashlight, which was a darn good idea. "Me?" he chuckled. "What are you doing here?"

"What does it look like?" she snapped. Yep, fear was well and truly gone. But the anger she was feeling was going to take a little longer before it disappeared.

"It looks like you're working a case that has already been solved." He raised a challenging eyebrow at her. "Tell me I'm wrong."

"Mr. Buck doesn't feel right —"

"Constance —"

"Listen will you!" she hurried, speaking over him so that he couldn't get a word in. "Look at this place." She gestured to the hidden quarry. "Who buries a body out here if they want it to be found? That's not to mention other... there are a whole bunch of... if you give me a minute, I'll explain..." The effect of the adrenaline pumping through her body was such that she wasn't able to think straight. She had so much to tell him, and didn't know where or how to begin.

"Are you finished?" he smirked.

"No!" She put her hands on her hips. "I want to speak to all the workers again. Tex-Mex, Piggly-Pete and Slim-Jim in particular. I want to know more about them, and Stu too. Honestly, this whole case has been a bit of a —"

"Constance." He didn't raise his voice, or even try and speak over her. Instead, he snapped her back into the moment with nothing more than the soft sounding of her name and what she took as a look of concern from the sheriff. She had been rambling, but the moment he spoke her name, she calmed down and trailed off. "Can I speak?" He asked.

"Fine," she agreed as she took a few deep breaths.

"I agree with you."

"..." Constance opened her mouth, but closed it. She was sure that she had misheard. Sheriff Nevil didn't agree with Constance. Sheriff Nevil didn't give her the benefit of the doubt. Sheriff Nevil didn't do much of anything but try and make her life a misery at every step. Yet Sheriff Nevil was grinning stupidly, looking just delighted in himself. "Come again?" she asked.

"I agree with you. Don't look so surprised." He crossed the last few steps to meet Constance. "I don't like Mr. Buck for the murderer. In fact, there's a lot I don't like. I think you're right. I think we need to —"

It sounded like a police siren, calling out in the distance, coming from over the trees and back toward the bypass. It was a loud, never ending wail, seeming to shake the trees and wake the night.

Sheriff Nevil cut off what he was saying immediately as he spun back to look in the direction of the noise. The two listened for a moment, trying to figure out what it was when realization dawned on Sheriff Nevil's face. "No, no, no!" he sprinted back across the quarry and toward the forest. "My car!"

Constance hurried after him, back up the sides of the quarry, through the forest and onto the bypass. It was easy enough to do this time, as she was able to use the wailing of the sirens to guide her. Although the closer she got, the more she came to realize that it wasn't a siren she was hearing, but a car alarm. And sure enough, as she breached the clearing, she spotted the source of the noise – a car in the midst of a panic attack.

If it wasn't such a sad sight, Constance just might have burst into laughter. Just like the last time, someone had gotten to Sheriff Nevil's car. This time however, it was his personal car; a red sports car of some make that Constance didn't know or care about. The front window had been broken, as had the side and back windows. The doors were smashed in too, and the roof had been caved in.

"Who would do this!" Sheriff Nevil wailed as he beat at the car like a father beating on the chest of his dead child. "Who?!" He fell to his knees, howling into the night.

Constance had to keep herself from laughing as she approached the beaten car. There was no spray-painted message that she could see, but she recognized the handiwork.

"See anything?" she asked as she spun around, looking up and down the length of the construction site. It was hard to identify if anything was amiss, as by now bodies began to pile from their trailers, all wondering what the cause of the noise was. Any one of them could have been the cause of the vandalism.

"Yes!" Sheriff Nevil cried. "My car is ruined!"

"Not that!" she hissed as she approached the hood. And that was when she saw it.

Underneath the windscreen wipers, among the broken pieces of glass, was a Polaroid photo, tucked in there as if by hand. Constance reached forward and gingerly plucked the photo free. She looked at the photo and gasped.

"What?" Sheriff Nevil had only just noticed what she was doing. "What's that?" She handed him the photo without looking. "Jesus," Sheriff Nevil said as he looked at the photo.

It was a photo of a dead body. Scrawled on the photo, beneath the body was the text 'He's not the guy. Stay off the case, or more will follow.'

So, Constance was right and Mr. Buck wasn't the killer. It was a relief in a way, a vindication of what she had known to be true this whole time. Yet, as great as it felt to be right, Constance just couldn't bring herself to get excited about it. Her work was only just beginning.

Chapter Sixteen

It was 6am in the small town of Modest Peak, and where Constance had never been one to sleep in, she had never been one to rise at the crack of dawn either. And yet, that's exactly what she was doing. She rose with the sun, had a quick shower, grabbed for herself a steaming hot coffee, and then wandered outside and onto the side of the road.

Sheriff Nevil was there already, waiting for her. He was leaning against an old police car; one that was free of damage. His face was balled up like he was about to start pitching a fit, and just like Constance, he looked tired.

"Nice car," she smirked as she reached the police vehicle and went for the front passenger door. "Does it come in red?"

"Don't," he warned as he climbed into the driver's seat. Constance didn't doubt that he was angry, but she felt that it was the unwarranted destruction of his car that had Sheriff Nevil in a state. So with this in mind, she chose not to take his short temper personally. It was far too early for such things.

Constance didn't press the issue with the car either, but it wasn't out of her feeling bad for him, or an attempt to ease the tension. None of that worried her one bit. Instead, she chose silence, simply so she could wake herself back up, and have another good long think on this case. It was turning into quite the doozy.

The two were headed out to the site again to give Foreman Joe the message that it needed to be shut down until further notice. There was no need for Constance to come along in order to give this message, but she had insisted.

"I want to see how they react," was all she said when pressed on why she was coming. The more and more she thought on it, the more she decided that the workers at the site were her most likely suspects. Best that she start keeping a closer eye on them.

"They'll react how I tell them," he grumbled to himself in response. Again, the car was still weighing on his mind.

There was more to this case then met the eye, and the insertion of what was possibly another dead body only made things weirder. Logic said that it was all the same person and that they wanted her off this case and were willing to do whatever it took... but only kind of.

The photo from the previous night was of a dead body, lying in the middle of an unidentifiable location. But that wasn't what was so odd.

The body in the photo was unrecognizable, but that seemed to be on purpose. Not only was their face cut out from the picture, but they weren't wearing any distinguishable clothes, or had anything else distinguishable about them. It was a body – from neck to ankles – with what must have been blood covering his chest, while his body lay on the ground... and that was about all that could be deduced from the picture.

There was something else a little off about the body too. And it wasn't the fake blood, or the way the photo had been taken, or anything like that. There was just something not right... but Constance was at a loss to figure out what it was. Every time she looked at the picture, she was certain she was missing something. But darn if she could figure it out.

One thing that both she and Sheriff Nevil both agreed on, upon further examination of the photo, was that it was more likely fake. And that was why it wasn't the pressing issue that it could have been. Not only was there no report of a missing person to link to the body, but there was no way of telling if the body was even dead.

"And Stu?" Constance had asked once this was decided upon.

"Stays locked up for now," Sheriff Nevil grumbled. "Just to make this whole thing a little easier to manage."

"And the site?" she pressed.

"Gets shut down."

The site was in full swing by the time Constance and Sheriff Nevil arrived. The sun had been up for less than thirty minutes, yet it looked as if the workers had been at it for hours... and hours. They were all working at an impossible rate, as if trying to make up for lost time. Even the sight of a police car pulling up barely caused pause.

"They're determined," Sheriff Nevil noted at the men as the hurried to and fro.

"Yeah... they are." Across the way, Constance spied Piggly-Pete. The most unfit of the entire crew, he, like everyone else, was working overtime. She'd never imagined the man could move at such a pace.

"What's he doing here – Jesus!" Sheriff Nevil barked.

Constance looked to where Sheriff Nevil was indicating, and wasn't at all surprised to see Mayor Brumbry there, speaking to Foreman Joe. She and the sheriff had every right to have been just a little shocked too. The man didn't live in Modest Peak, and really had no reason to be at the site. And yet there he was, clear as day, conversing with Foreman Joe like he was running the show.

Again, Constance probably should have been surprised by the sight of the mayor, but she just couldn't be. The man had such a personal investment in the bypass that one would think it was his own money going into the thing. Maybe it was... for the smallest inkling of a second, Constance had a mind to do some digging on the mayor. He was rather invested in this case after all...

But the sound of Sheriff Nevil opening his door and striding from the car snapped her back into the moment. Before she had so much as undone her own belt, he was already halfway toward the mayor and foreman. "Hey! Wait!" Constance shouted as she tried, and failed, to hurry after him.

"... don't tell me how to do my job," Sheriff Nevil was saying to the mayor as Constance came in beside them. "I've given my reasons, and that should be enough."

"I'm not trying to tell you anything." Mayor Brumbry was starting to look frustrated, and more than that even. He was fidgeting with his hands, moving his feet and looking every which way as he searched for a means by which to dismiss Sheriff Nevil. "I just don't see what one has to do with the other."

"Again, it doesn't matter what you think," Sheriff Nevil said patiently. "It honestly doesn't concern you one bit."

"What's going on?" Constance asked as she inserted herself beside Sheriff Nevil.

"It's not important," Sheriff Nevil dismissed.

"Maybe not for you!" Mayor Brumbry exclaimed. "But I need this bypass finished and I hate to say it – no, no, I do. But I just do not get the feeling that you appreciate the urgency here."

"Urgency!" Sheriff Nevil looked ready to explode. "I'm trying to solve a murder."

"And you solved it!"

"I don't think so." Sheriff Nevil was shaking, so Constance touched at his arm to calm him down. "Despite what I may have said yesterday... things have changed."

"What? Because of some picture?" Mayor Brumbry cried.

"What picture?" Foreman Joe asked from behind the mayor.

"It's not important," the mayor dismissed.

"It is important," Sheriff Nevil shot back. "More than you think. Which is why this whole site needs to be shut down until —"

"But the blood-stained vest!" Mayor Brumbry cut in again. "You found it in his house!" He wrung his hands in the air in desperation.

"And it's being taken into account. Along with a lot of other things. I'm sorry, Mayor Brumbry, but you're not going to change my mind." Sheriff Nevil crossed his arms and did his best to give a "this conversation is over" impression.

"Ms. Aberfield?" the mayor had turned to her now, eyes pleading, desperation seeping from his every pore. "And you agree with this?" For some reason he seemed to think that Constance would be on his side, and more than that, that she would then be able to change Sheriff Nevil's mind..

"I do," she offered simply. Although, her reasons for thinking so were anything but simple.

Mayor Brumbry looked just about ready to explode. Chest puffed up, face turning red, Constance was only too ready for him to try and assert his 'dominance' over Sheriff Nevil and get the man to change his mind. She knew that this would never work of course, so she was very much looking forward to it.

But then the mayor deflated, exhaled and tried a completely different approach. "Look, maybe we can talk about this? In private?"

"I don't see why that would make a difference."

"Please," he pleaded. He reached out to touch Sheriff Nevil's arm, but then retracted. "Maybe we can get breakfast and you can lay out why it needs to be closed. And I can offer my counter arguments. How's that sound?"

"There really is no point."

"Please, Sheriff."

Surprisingly, Sheriff Nevil looked to Constance for confirmation. She knew that it would be a pointless endeavor, but she also knew it was near impossible to say no to the mayor when he really wanted a yes. Therefore, she shrugged a 'why not?' and Sheriff Nevil agreed.

"Perfect!" Mayor Brumbry clapped his hands together as if he had won a great victory. He then turned to Foreman Joe and spoke softly to him. "Go and wait in your trailer – do it. I'll come back as soon as I am done with the Sheriff."

Foreman Joe looked very much like he was going to say no, most likely just because he didn't like being spoken down to or told what to do. But then he met the mayor's eyes and something in them told him to obey. A second later and he was nodding his head and lumbering back across the site and toward his trailer.

Constance watched the exchange between the two men with some curiosity. She had spoken with Foreman Joe twice now, and both times he had seemed to get off on being in a position of power over her. Whether it was his physical dominance, or just the fact that she had needed something from him, he had thoroughly enjoyed being the one in charge. She had sensed at the time that this was a common personality trait of the big man, and was thus shocked to see him submit so easily to Mayor Brumbry. But there was also more.

Just the exchange in general, and how close the two men seemed. She knew that the mayor was the one commissioning this bypass, but did that mean he needed to be on personal terms with the workers? Not to mention showing up to the site daily and making sure everything was a go. There was no way that was normal.

She remained standing where she was, watching Foreman Joe as he disappeared inside his trailer. And even after he was gone, she stayed put, staring at the place he had just been until —

"Constance? Constance?" Sheriff Nevil called from his car. "Are you coming?"

"Huh..." Constance blinked herself back into the moment, only to realize that she was alone. Sheriff Nevil had since left her, having headed back toward his car, and Mayor Brumbry was even further away as he too hurried to his own car.

"Are you coming?" Sheriff Nevil asked again.

"Right." She gave her head a shake and hurried to the car. As she reached the passenger door, she paused and looked to Sheriff Nevil. "Can you drop me off at home, Rog?"

"Why? Not in the mood to hear the mayor list his reasons why a bypass being built is more important than a murder case?"

"It sounds like fun... but I've got somewhere I need to be."

"Where?" Sheriff Nevil frowned as he popped his door open and climbed into the driver's seat.

"Denver," Constance answered as she too climbed into the front passenger seat and buckled herself in. "I've got to go to Denver."

Chapter Seventeen

There was something fishy going on with Mayor Brumbry. Constance didn't know how fishy exactly, nor did she know to what extent this fishiness effected the case, if at all. What she did know was that Mayor Brumbry was acting strange and it was up to her to find out why.

It had started with him coming to her to work the case. At the time it had seemed fair enough as he wanted the case solved and thought that she'd be the best person to make sure that happened. What she hadn't really taken into account was how eager he was to have the case solved. She had assumed him to just want the murderer apprehended, something that she couldn't really blame him for. But now that she really thought about it, he didn't really seem at all concerned about the actual committing of the murder. Just that it affected the bypass.

That was all the mayor seemed to care about. It had been nothing but 'bypass this' and 'bypass that' since she had met him. He had scheduled that town meeting the night before Stu had died, and had spent nearly every waking minute in Modest Peak since. And again, it was never out of respect for Stu, but rather to ensure that the bypass got finished.

And then there was the way he had been speaking to Foreman Joe earlier. Again, it wasn't anything too nefarious or obvious. It was just... well, it was strange. She could understand Foreman Joe wanting construction to keep going, but why were they coordinating as if they both had equal stakes in the bypass?

All of this wasn't to say that Mayor Brumbry had killed Stu, not at all. But it was beyond obvious that the mayor had some sort of personal investment in this bypass and Constance wanted to know what. Surely it was more than just his desire to see a bump in the polls.

It was for these reasons that Constance decided it was time to do a little digging on the Mayor of Denver. And it was her desire to do some digging that saw her make the two-hour drive to Denver after leaving the construction site, and then head straight for his office. Lucky then that she had nothing but time on her hands.

"Hey there!" Mayor Brumbry's secretary beamed as Constance walked through the door. She was a young woman, nearly a girl by Constance's personal standards, with big blue eyes, blonde hair, a very pretty face and a lot of other physical attributes that would have made her appealing to the superficial male. "How may I, and the Mayor of Denver, help you today?" Her voice was high-pitched, almost childlike.

The waiting room to the office was a small space, only just capable of fitting a couple of waiting chairs, a reception desk and a water fountain. Honestly, it was a lot smaller than Constance would have assumed... and a lot shabbier.

"Hello," Constance started casually as she approached the reception. The receptionist – name tag reading Mandy – blinked and smiled. She was dull, and obviously a little slow. Constance figured this to be a good thing. "Is the mayor in?"

"Not today I'm afraid," she beamed but didn't continue.

"And he is..." Constance pressed.

"Oh! He's overseeing the Mid-West Bypass, personally. As of right now he is in..." she flipped through her diary. "A lovely little town called Modest Peak." She looked up to Constance and blinked again.

So, he wasn't lying about where he was, that was a good thing, at least for the mayor. It meant he wasn't trying to hide anything, which further implied his innocence. But that didn't mean he was completely innocent in all of this.

"He's rather fond of this bypass, isn't he?" Constance pressed as she leaned on the reception desk. "Tell me, is it normal for a mayor to be so... hands on?"

"Normal?" Mandy blinked innocently.

Constance was about to respond, when she took another quick look around the office, looked back at Mandy... and then straight back to the walls of the small space. She had seen posters covering the walls when she'd first walked in, but had glanced over them. She had rightfully assumed them just to be standard campaign posters and the like. They were not.

There were over twenty posters covering the walls – large and medium in size – and every single one concerned the bypass. There were simple posters, with just a map of where the bypass was going to go, and there were more elaborate ones with Mayor Brumbry out on the site, building the bypass by himself. This guy really, really, really wanted this bypass to happen. And more than that, he wanted everyone to know he was involved.

"Say..." Constance started slowly as she pulled her eyes from the posters and looked back to Mandy – still blinking and smiling merrily. "This bypass? Is there a reason that Mayor Brumbry is so... determined?"

"Determined?" Mandy frowned and blinked her big blue eyes like an innocent puppy. "It's his biggest campaign promise."

"Yes... but why?" Constance asked through gritted teeth. Was this woman purposefully dense, or was she really that slow?

"Oh!" Mandy's eyes popped and she clapped her hands together. "Because he's losing in the polls of course. He thinks this will help boost his numbers." She sounded happy.

"Losing? By how much?"

"At least ten points!" She could not have sounded more excited... but that was probably just because she was thrilled to be able to answer a question for a change.

"And what? This bypass is meant to give him a bump?"

"Eleven points!" she cried. "At least that's what analysts say. People love jobs. Job, jobs, jobs! Is there anything else?" she finished confidently.

"And when is the election?"

"Three months – eighty-seven days and counting."

Constance had been right. Mayor Brumbry was just as invested in the bypass as she'd assumed, and for good reason. He needed it finished before the election in three months if he was to have any hope of being reelected and keeping his job. But was that enough to kill over? And how would killing Stu have helped in any way?

Mysteries could be as frustrating as they were scintillating. For every new answer received, two new questions were sure to pop up. And where this would have been fine, had Constance known that she was asking the right questions, there was no way of possibly knowing that. For all she knew she was chasing her tail, rather than anything remotely involved in the case.

Feeling more frustrated now than anything, Constance was rather short in her goodbye to Mandy. But just because she was frustrated, didn't mean she was going to give up. After Mayor Brumbry's office, she still had one other place she wanted to stop by.

Stu lived in Denver.... which was strange enough in itself. From his unit block to where the bypass started, was a little more than a two-hour drive. And yet, due to his own insecurities and fears, he refused to make that drive every day and insisted in being put up at a hotel.

"He doesn't like long drives," Sheriff Nevil had explained to Constance when she had first heard this. "Claims he's prone to micro-sleeps."

"Fun guy," she had mused at the time. It was said with extreme sarcasm of course, for everything she had since learned about Stu indicated that he was the complete opposite of a 'fun guy.' This belief was further confirmed by the contents of his apartment.

Stu was a nerd. There was just no other way to put it. From his decor, to his DVD collection, right on through to the clothing he wore, he was a straight up geek. His clothes were all bright colors with superhero emblems and puns about geography on them. His DVD collection was stocked with nature documentaries and films with characters like 'Iron Man' and 'The Green Lantern' in them – although Constance could only guess what the heck that meant. And instead of books, he had comics.

"So, Stu considers himself a superhero," Constance mused as she stepped through his small apartment, eyeing the posters of superheroes that covered every square inch.

But there weren't just posters of these caped crusaders. There were photos too, with Stu in them, dressed in a superhero outfit. Constance frowned as she picked up a series of small snapshots of Stu at some sort of convention. So many photos of Stu and his hobbies... but none of his friends.

The lack of other people in his life was a constant theme, present throughout Stu's apartment. And the more that Constance looked through his comic collection, his rock collection – no fooling, an actual rock collection – and his DVD collection all stored in an order that Constance could not work out, she realized that Stu was a bit of a loner.

She made her way into the kitchen, still with thoughts of Stu's apparent lack of friends. This lifestyle contrasted pretty heavily with what Tex-Mex, Slim-Jim and Piggly-Pete had to say. They all considered themselves best buds. At the time, Constance had had no choice but to believe them... but now she thought otherwise. There was just no way that those three would befriend a guy like Stu. No way at all.

About to leave the kitchen, Constance's eye caught sight of a diary sitting by the home telephone. She shrugged as she reached for it and flipped in open. She didn't expect to find anything interesting, an expectation that was confirmed as she flipped back the previous week... and then the next week... and then the week after that. Stu lived a very dull life. Maybe even more dull than that? Again, she was forced to consider the very real possibility that she had been lied to by the construction workers and that they were not, by any stretch of the imagination, Stu's friends.

Bored with the diary, she was about to put it down when she flipped to a page that was hard to miss. Big red text covered the center of the page, taking up over half of its space. It was a simple message, but underlined several times so as to show its importance. 'Happy Birthday to me.'

Stu's birthday was over one month ago. Constance smirked to herself as this fact dawned upon her. In isolation, it really wasn't that interesting, especially now that he was passed. But when considering what she had been told by Tex-Mex, Slim-Jim and Piggly-Pete, it took on a whole new meaning.

She had heard those three arguing with Stu the night before he disappeared. Although she hadn't heard what the argument was about, each to the last had claimed that it was in regards to his birthday party. It now appeared that wasn't the case. The three had been lying to Constance. No doubt they had come up with it earlier, thinking it to be a lie that would make them sound even more holy then they already appeared to be. Unfortunately, they were too stupid to double check its truth.

Tex-Mex, Slim-Jim and Piggly-Pete were not Stu's friends. Even more than that, they may have been his enemies. Constance had no idea what they had been arguing about the night before Stu died, but she was willing to bet that it didn't make those three look particularly good. But, was it enough to commit murder over? Constance was going to find out.

Chapter Eighteen

Stu lived on the top floor of a thirty-five-story apartment complex. And where the view was lovely, the elevator was also broken.

Standing at the top of the stairwell, Constance looked down its many flights as they curved around the interior of the building. As she took a deep breath and began her decent, she was want to admit that this was going to take her some time. It was lucky then that she needed it to think.

She was so close to figuring this case out, she could feel it. All she needed now was the link, that single piece of evidence that got this case rolling. If solving a crime was like putting together a puzzle, then all she needed was a glimpse at the front of the box, just to give her some indication as to what she was meant to be putting together. Once she had that, she was sure she'd be well on her way.

The annoying thing was that she had all the pieces. There were the townspeople and their oppressive tirade to stop her from investigating the crime. In their zeal they had staged a false assault in a bid to scare her off. Whether they were linked to the murder though, she still wasn't sure.

There were the construction workers, the 'big three' in particular that had recently moved to the head of the suspect list. Where they had claimed to be close to Stu, Constance was now certain this to be a falsehood. Furthermore, she had seen them arguing with Stu the night before he disappeared. Finding out what this argument was about was at the top of her list.

Next came Mayor Brumbry, the eager civil servant that was just a touch too involved in a situation that didn't really involve him. Of everyone, he had the most to lose from Constance not solving this case. At least that was how it seemed. Yet despite this, she still didn't want to rule him out completely. There was more there, and she was going to find out what.

And then there were the miscellaneous bits of evidence. There was the blood-stained vest that just happened to be – and very luckily so – in Mr. Buck's bedroom, lain out on the bed as if on display. And where this should have been enough to convict Mr. Buck, the arrival of a new dead body and a message, all but cleared him.

Constance was nearing the bottom of the stairwell, but she knew that if she didn't stop to take a break she might just fall the rest of the way. And sure, that would save her some time, but the broken bones received probably wouldn't be worth it. As such, she pulled herself up and leaned against the railing to cool down. And as she got about cooling, she reached into her coat pocket and plucked out a copy of the photo of the dead body... the apparently dead body.

Constance had seen a lot of dead bodies in her time and she was pretty sure that this wasn't one. First of all, there were no apparent wounds, just a lot of blood. Like, too much blood. So much blood that the person staging it had clearly never seen a murder before. Second, the way the photo was taken was just off. The body's head was cut off from the photo, as were his feet, and there was something not right about the way he was lying either.

For the hundredth time since first seeing the picture, Constance squinted her eyes and focused in on the photo, on that body. The location was non-descript, but the way that the body was lying on its back, the angle of its legs... there was something about it that Constance just could not place.

It was for all of those reasons that the photo of the body was only being taken half-seriously, if that. It was enough to stall the conviction of Mr. Buck, but it wasn't enough to let him off entirely.

Taking a deep breath, Constance shoved the photo back in her pocket and got about taking the rest of the stairs. It was going to take her another two minutes at least to finish the journey. After that, it was a long two-hour drive back to Modest Peak. It was a drive that Constance wasn't looking forward to, especially as she was sure that come the end of it she would be even more confused than before.

The parking lot was located underneath the building, in what amounted to a huge concrete cage. As Constance breached the door and started to make her way across the vast, open space, she barely bothered a glance around. That was how in her own head she was. Her car was located across the other side, and as a few of the lights were out, she had to walk in the dark for much of it. Again, none of this registered-on Constance as she was far too preoccupied.

It was on account of this total lack of spatial awareness that Constance didn't hear the sound of hurried footsteps as they approached her from behind. And she certainly didn't notice the shadow either as it stretched out beneath her, indicating that someone was right behind. It wasn't until a pair of hands had wrapped themselves around Constance's mouth to silence her, and then spun her around on the spot that she finally noticed she was being followed. And by then, it was far too late.

"Don't say a word. Not one." The man was wearing a black balaclava, his breath smelled of cigarettes, and his voice was deep. Naturally deep though, not put on or exaggerated.

Constance didn't respond. She couldn't. With the hand held over her mouth, it was all she could do to breathe, let alone scream.

"Good." His face was inches from her own, which only made the smell that much worse. Constance tried to twist her head away so as to avoid the wafts of cigarette that drifted from his mouth, but he held her head firm so she couldn't move. "Now, listen here. You're going to get back in this car, drive back to that little crappy town and arrest Mr. Buck for good. He killed Stu. He's guilty. So arrest him and be done with it. Understand?"

Constance's lack of response to the question had nothing to do with the fact that she couldn't have responded, even if she had wanted to. It was more to do with surprise, than anything else. He wanted Constance to arrest Stu? Was that what he had said? But that didn't make any sense.

"Understand?" he growled after another moment, when Constance didn't respond.

"Hhhmmmfffhhh," Constance mumbled from underneath his hand.

"What?"

"Hmmfffgggmmm," she tried again, even shrugging so as to emphasize the point.

The man in the balaclava groaned, glanced around the parking lot so as to make sure it was empty and then slowly took his hand from Constance's mouth. "Now? What do you say?"

"I don't understand..." she started.

"What don't you —"

"You want me to arrest Mr. Buck? So, you want me to finish this case off?"

"Yes!" he snarled. "And quickly. Today. If you don't, I'll kill you."

"Yes, yes," she dismissed. "I'm sure you will. But are you sure you don't mean to tell me that you want me to drop the case? Not finish it?"

"Huh? No, I said arrest Stu. Or else!" He shoved his face right into Constance, glaring at her with as much menace as he most likely could.

Constance wasn't in the least bit worried. Oh sure, this man was threatening her life, but it was all in a day's works by now. And besides... she didn't believe for a minute that he meant it.

What had her confused was the mixed messaging. The last time she had been accosted like this, the demand was to drop the case entirely. It was this demand that had her sure it was the townspeople involved in the case. And of not the case, then the attack. But this guy wanted Stu arrested. Logic implied that this was a different attacker. And she was sure that her previous attacker had been a non-smoker too! But there was only way to be sure.

Constance looked for her moment and found it a second later when the entrance door to the parking lot opened across the way and a large man waddled through the door and spotted the man in the balaclava attacking Constance.

"Hey!" the large man shouted out. "What's going on?!

The man in the balaclava spun back when he heard the man shout, taking his eyes off Constance for the first time. The second he did, Constance lifted back her right leg and drove her foot into her attacker's shin with as much force as she possibly could.

"Yaaooooowww!" the man in the balaclava screeched as he let go of Constance and grabbed onto his shin. His voice cracked as he screamed, but it remained just as deep. This man was not the same that had attacked her previously.

"Are you okay?!" The large man called as he waddled across the way and toward Constance.

By now, the man in the balaclava was making a run for it... kind of. Constance must have kicked him harder than she had realized, because the man in the balaclava didn't so much as run, but limp. "Arrest Mr. Buck," he shouted over his shoulder as he bypassed the large man with ease. "Today!"

As the large man hurried to check on Constance, making sure that she was okay, Constance watched the man in the balaclava hobble away. The way he moved, with a stiff leg and wide gait, reminded her of Mr. Buck and the way he walked. Although it obviously wasn't Mr. Buck, as the man was in jail. And it was as she though came to mind that a sudden realization struck Constance like a bolt of lightning.

"Ma'am?" the large man checked again.

Constance didn't respond. Her hand shot into her jacket pocket and pulled out the photo of the 'dead' body. Something had been bothering her about that photo and now she knew what it was. The dead body had an extremely stiff, straightened right leg, much like Mr. Buck.

She squinted at the dead body, from the neck down to the leg. There could be no doubt now that the body was Mr. Buck's, and that someone – although it wasn't hard to guess who, and that 'someone' was most likely "someones" – had faked his murder and taken a photo. And where this probably should have raised more questions than it answered, like the final puzzle falling into place, Constance knew fully well what it meant.

"Ma'am?" the large man tried a third time.

Constance thanked the man for his help and assured him that she was okay. After that, she jumped in her car and started the trip back to Modest Peak. On the way, she had a few phone calls to make and a meeting to organize. It was time to get to the bottom of this once and for all.

Chapter Nineteen

The first thing that Constance did was to call up Sheriff Nevil and have him release Mr. Buck. Sheriff Nevil was obviously against this idea, as the man was a possible murderer, but Constance assured him that it was necessary. This was made all the harder by the fact that she was driving back to Modest Peak at a very fast pace, having to dodge between traffic while trying to not get herself killed. Why couldn't he just go along one time without having to argue?!

"And what if he decides to kill again?" Sheriff Nevil pointed out when Constance continued to pester him.

"Do you really think that Mr. Buck is our man?" she asked dryly.

"Well... no I don't —"

"Then what are you complaining about? Look, if it makes you feel any better, I know exactly where he's going to go once he's released. You can come along and keep an eye on him. Make sure that the old man with a bung right foot doesn't go on a spree."

There was a pause on the line after this comment, one which Constance was certain was dedicated to Sheriff Nevil cursing her under his breath. "And where exactly is he going?" Sheriff Nevil finally asked.

Constance answered the question, while also trying not to give too much away. She loved the fact that she had solved a part of the case and wanted to see Sheriff Nevil's face when she revealed it.

Once she was done with Sheriff Nevil, she put in her next call. This one was to Dakota.

"Constance!" Dakota beamed down the line. "Where are you – are you in the building?"

"What? No – Look, I need a favor. Can you —"

"What favor?"

"If you'll let me talk, I can tell you. All right?" Constance waited for Dakota to respond, when she didn't, she continued. "I need you to —"

"To what?" Dakota burst on the other end of the line.

"Will you just listen!" Constance snapped. As she yelled, she realized that her foot was pressed flat on the accelerator. She quickly eased it up, slowing down the car just a touch.

"I am," Dakota announced.

Constance paused, and then continued. "I need you to organize a meeting for one hour from now. Just between you and —"

"With who?" Dakota cut in again. This time, Constance ignored her as she continued to speak.

"You, your brother, Mr. Trunch and Mr. Buck. It's about —"

"Mr. Buck is in prison," Dakota pointed out. "I don't think he'll be able to —"

"He's being released as we speak." Another paused, waiting for Dakota to cut in. When she didn't Constance continued. "So, it's you, your brother, Mr. Trunch and Mr. Buck. The hotel will do, I just need them together so I can —"

"What for?" Dakota asked excitedly.

Constance seethed. "It's to do with the bypass. I know a way to stop it from being built, forever. But I need all hands on deck. Understand?"

"Constance?! Seriously?! You figured something out?!"

"I did." Constance hated lying, especially to someone she considered a friend. But desperate times called for these types of circumstances, and besides, she figured that once the meeting was done, they'd forget the reason they were called anyway. "Can you do that, Dakota?"

"I'm on it." She sounded serious for perhaps the first time in her life, and Constance half imagined her saluting, as if she were in the army.

"I'll see you in an hour." And then Constance hung up the phone.

Constance could have kicked herself for not seeing it sooner. She blamed the fact that she had been out of the game for so long, that she was a little rusty and this was likely the reason that she had taken a little longer to put the pieces together than she once would have. But even still... she should have seen it all so much earlier.

The people of Modest Peak had nothing to do with the murder of Stu. That much, she was now certain of. But regardless of this fact, they weren't completely blameless in all of this, and had committed their own crimes that they would need to be reprimanded for. That was what she was on her way to do now. She was going to call them out, have them confess, and then finally put her mind to solving a murder. That was the point of all of this in the first place.

It was an hour later when Constance pulled her car up to the front curb just outside The Lone Peak Hotel. Sheriff Nevil's beaten and battered police car was parked there also, looking about as miserable as a car could. She was pleased to see it parked though, as it meant he had arrived. If he hadn't, she would have had to have started without him.

As Constance hustled her way down the path and toward the entrance, she ran over in her head what she was going to say and how she was going to say it. She had spent the last hour trying to figure this out and still wasn't one hundred percent sure what she was going to say exactly. She knew she needed to be firm and in control. She knew she needed to be harsh, hard and speak to the point. She knew she needed to let them all know that she knew for a fact what she was speaking of, regardless of their denial. She knew everything... expect for what she was going to say.

But she also figured that she could just wing it. Improv was often the best way to go about these things, as it often came off sounding far more natural. A small kick to her step as she reached the door, threw it open and burst inside.

All the key players were already in the lobby, sitting around on the couches and leaning against the walls as they waited for her. There was Dakota and Dexter, standing by reception, both looking particularly excited. There was Mr. Trunch standing in the corner, arms folded, looking cautious. There was Mr. Buck pacing back and forth, dragging his leg, looking about as angry as always. And there was Sheriff Nevil, seated on the couch, leg bobbing up and down, waiting impatiently.

At the sight of Constance walking into the room, all eyes and bodies turned on her. Sheriff Nevil was the first to speak, pushing himself up from the couch and striding to meet Constance.

"Constance!" Sheriff Nevil started. "What is going —"

"Is it true!?" Dexter called as he hurried to meet her. "Dakota said —"

"You know how to stop the bypass?" Mr. Trunch barked. "That's what she said."

"You better not be lying," Mr. Buck sneered. "I don't like liars."

Constance didn't answer any of them. Not at first, anyway. Instead she made her way to the middle of the room and stood so that everyone else was forced to surround her. They were like crows, circling a fresh corpse, waiting until their time to feast. As they eyed her, she turned and looked at each one, making sure that all their attention was on her. And then, she started.

"I lied." She spoke with her chin pointed high, as if she were proud of what she had to say. "I don't have a way to save the bypass."

"What?!" the entire room, save Sheriff Nevil, exclaimed in unison.

"But that doesn't matter," she continued. "Believe me, you all have much bigger things to worry —"

"What's the meaning of this, Constance?" Mr. Trunch growled. "You called us here specifically – specifically because you said you have a way to stop the bypass."

"I knew she was lying," Mr. Buck snarled. "First she breaks into my house, second she has me framed and third —"

"Constance, tell us it isn't so!" Dakota pleaded. "Please!?"

Constance smirked as she reached into her pocket and plucked out the photo of the fake dead body. She then turned and handed it to Mr. Buck. "I believe you'll be wanting this."

Mr. Buck took the photo with some caution, as if worried it might bite him. "Why would I want this?"

"Well, it's you, isn't it?" There, the way his eyes popped all but shouted his guilt for Constance to hear. "I must say, you look rather good for a dead man."

"I don't... I'm not..." he blathered and stuttered.

"What are you implying, Constance?" Mr. Trunch asked. He had his arms crossed over his chest, fixing her with such a look of defiance that one would think she was accusing him of faking his death.

"This." She took one short stride toward Dexter, lifted her right leg back and drove her foot into Dexter's shin. The effect was instantaneous.

"Oww!!!!!" Dexter screamed as he grabbed at his shin and started jumping on the spot. The wail was high-pitched and perfectly in tune, just like that of the mugger from the other night.

"Constance!" Dakota gaped as she hurried to comfort her hobbled brother. "What are you doing?!"

"I was attacked in Denver, not two hours ago." As she spoke, she turned on the spot, making sure that each and every single person was watching her. They were, of course. Each to the last looked guilty as sin... except for Sheriff Nevil. He smirked and nodded his head, as if he knew where she was going. "The man who attacked me wasn't the same one from the other night."

Mr. Trunch still had his arms crossed, still had his chest puffed, and was still trying to look innocent. "I don't know what you're trying to —"

"I thought to myself," she continued over him. "What are the odds of being attacked by two different men? Both dressed the same. Both with similar demands. Astronomical!"

"If what you say is true, then it couldn't have possibly been any of us," Mr. Trunch continued. "We've been here for over thirty minutes."

"Who said it was any of you?" she asked with a smirk. "But thanks for making that leap. No, no, the man who attacked me wasn't one of you. Don't worry about that. But the point I'm trying to make is that he made me realize something." A pause. "All these random attacks weren't committed by the same person, but the same persons. You." She indicated to the group so that her meaning couldn't be misconstrued.

As expected, the group of four acted appropriately shocked at her suggestion. They stuttered, they stumbled and they tripped over themselves as they tried to deny her. The only one who didn't appear shocked was Sheriff Nevil.

"We didn't kill anyone!" Dakota exclaimed in a panic. "We didn't!"

"I know that," Constance assured her. "Even you, Mr. Buck I am sure to be innocent. Of murder anyway. But that doesn't mean you didn't take advantage. If you're guilty of anything, it's that."

"Advantage?" Mr. Buck asked. "What do you —"

"All four of you want this bypass to end. Better, you want it to have never begun in the first place. When the body of Stu turned up, and Sheriff Nevil announced that the bypass would be stopped until further notice, you all saw an opportunity to get your way." She turned on Dexter. "You attacked me in the street, and warned me to stay off the case."

"I did not!" he cried.

She then turned on Mr. Trunch. "And you vandalized Sheriff Nevil's car when we were interviewing Dexter. You all knew we'd go right to Dexter and Dakota, so you decided to use that to your advantage and imply we were following the wrong lead. Clever."

Mr. Trunch didn't say anything. Rather, he looked appropriately guilty as he stared at his feet, body deflating.

"And as for that photo? I don't know when you took it, or even when you intended to use it. But after Mr. Buck was arrested, you figured that to be as good a time as any. Not only would it force us to reconsider his innocence, but it would shut the bypass down again." She turned on the spot, trying and failing to meet their eyes. Each person to the last was now staring at their feet. "The four of you worked together to disrupt this investigation. And although you didn't kill anyone, you made sure that myself and Sheriff Nevil were chasing our tails instead of the correct leads. You should all be ashamed of yourself."

The atmosphere in the room was morose. Dexter, Dakota, Mr. Trunch and Mr. Buck all stared at their feet, kicking the ground and refusing to look up and meet Constance's accusatory stare. No doubt they hadn't stopped to think of the big picture – that they were aiding a murderer.

"We're sorry!" Dakota suddenly burst into tears. "We're sorry!"

"Quiet girl!" Mr. Buck snapped.

"We didn't mean to! Honest!" It was Dexter now, crying as hard and ferociously as his sister. "We just wanted to stop the bypass from happening. That's all! We didn't think it would... that the murderer... we never..."

And that was that. Constance crossed her arms and looked around the small group. "Sheriff Nevil?" Constance continued. "I assume you'll want to be having a word with them?"

"Yeah. I do." Sheriff Nevil didn't look pleased, although Constance guessed that was more to do with the state of his car than the actual investigation which they had disrupted. "The station. All of you. Now!"

The four kept their heads bowed as they turned and began their march toward the front door. Constance watched them go, beaming to herself over a job well done.... well, half a job anyway. As satisfying as it was to finally figure out who it had been that attacked her, vandalized those cars and planted the photo of a fake-dead body, Constance could only enjoy the moment so much.

Up until an hour ago, she was almost certain that the attacks, the vandalism and the murder were all linked. She was sure that once she figured out who was behind one, the rest of the case would fall into place. But that wasn't to be. All she had really managed to do was wipe the townspeople from her list of suspects.

In fact, the case was in an even worse spot than it was before. Where once she had a whole list of possible suspects, she now had none. As much as she hated admitting it, the townspeople were her key suspects for most of the investigation, and now that they were out of the case, she wasn't sure what she was going to do. , scratch that. She was pretty certain who she was going to look into next, she just didn't know by which means she was going to do it.

"Constance?" Sheriff Nevil asked from the doorway. He had followed the group out the door, most likely directing them to his car so as to head to the station. "Are you coming along?"

"No," she said slowly. "You can take care of that. I've got something else I need to do."

She had expected Sheriff Nevil to argue, but to her surprise he simply nodded, turned and exited the hotel. Alone now, and with that ugly chapter behind her, it was time for Constance to finally get about solving a murder. Wasn't that the point of this whole thing in the first place?

Chapter Twenty

It was lucky that Constance knew Modest Peak like the back of her hand. If she hadn't, then she would have found it rather difficult to have tracked down the men she was searching for and then watch them like a hawk, all while remaining hidden from view. But she did know Modest Peak like the back of her hand, and as such, she was able to track down the men she was looking for, and remain hidden from view, without too much concern or worry.

Truth be told, it was rather easy to find these men, and little, if any, local knowledge was needed. When Constance left her hotel, after having the townspeople admit fault for what they had done, it was just getting past three in the afternoon. The bypass was currently closed down on orders of Sheriff Nevil, and as such there was only one place that her targets could possibly be.

The targets in question were Tex-Mex, Slim-Jim and Piggly-Pete, and as the three men were known degenerates – at least they were degenerates as far as Constance was concerned – the only place they could possibly be was the bar next door, The Loner. Constance took a hard right out of her hotel and hurried toward the entrance to The Loner, certain she would find the three men within its seedy depths.

Oh, how she hated The Loner. She hated everything about it. She hated the decor – or lack thereof. She hated the owner. She hated the smell. She hated the atmosphere. She hated how the wooden floor creaked and groaned with each step taken. She hated that the air was so darn smoky that she could barely breathe. She hated it all and where it under any other circumstance, she would have never been caught dead inside. But it wasn't any other circumstance and it was because of this that Constance took a deep breath, held her head up high and stepped inside without delay.

If Constance was being perfectly honest with herself, the bar wasn't that bad, and had she been anyone else then she might have liked the place. Unfortunately, she and the bar's owner, Eustace, had a rather tumultuous relationship which had long ago soured her opinion of the bar. The moment that she entered she could feel Eustace's eyes on her, watching her with suspicion as she crept through the establishment, eyes searching for her targets.

The bar was rather busy for three in the afternoon; packed to the rafters, in fact. This no doubt had everything to do with the bypass being closed until further notice, as every single patron looked to be a construction worker. Constance's eyes scanned the bar until she spotted the three men she was after. They sat in the back corner, drinking and laughing the day away. No doubt they were beyond pleased with the current circumstance, as they would be getting paid regardless of whether they worked or not.

Constance tried to remain as inconspicuous as possible as she made her way closer and closer, eventually taking a seat just behind the three men; close enough so that she could hear fragments of their conversation, but not so close so that it would be obvious she was watching them. Indeed, they didn't so much as glance in her direction as she sat down. They carried on as they always did; drinking, laughing and being all around pests, blissfully unaware that Constance was on to them.

The more that Constance thought about it, the more certain she became that one of these three men was behind the murder of Stu. They just had to be!

Not only had she seen them with Stu the night before his murder – bullying him, no less – but they were just really bad guys; total jerks, to be perfectly frank. Constance had a pretty good gut instinct too, and right now it was screaming that one of these three was responsible.

But which one could it be? As Constance sunk into her chair, making sure to remain hidden, she got about trying to separate the three men, trying to decide which was the most loathsome, the most likely to kill someone. This proved harder than she would have thought. First of all, the bar was so darn noisy that she could barely hear a word spoken. There was a lot of cursing and shouting and laughing, but nothing distinguishable. And secondly, and as far as she was concerned, all three were prime candidates.

Tex-Mex was the clear leader of the group. From his annoyingly handsome face, to his arrogant smirk, to the way that the other two hung off his every word, it was clear that when he said 'jump,' they asked 'how high.' Slim-Jim looked to be the comedic one; everything he said was followed by bouts of laughter and pats on the back. And Piggly-Pete was the hanger-on, the kind of guy that was just happy to have two friends that didn't mind him hanging around. Honestly, the odds were that he did the deed just to try and impress the other two.

For Constance, this was the 'boring' part of the investigative process. It was a lot of sitting and waiting, hoping to be inspired or to learn something new. Sometimes it worked a treat, and often it didn't. After twenty minutes of sitting and listening, Constance was no closer to figuring anything else out. She had found her suspects, but could feel time slipping away, being wasted as she sat there and did what amounted to twiddling her thumbs. Annoyed at herself, and feeling frustrated, she was about to get up and leave when the three men suddenly pushed back their seats and stood.

Constance was quick to slink back into her chair, even going to far as to cover her face as the three lumbered past her. Again, she tried to listen to what was being said, but got nothing. The moment they were out the door, Constance was up on her feet. Her plan was to follow them in whatever they did, never letting them out of her sight, sticking to them like glue until a new piece of evidence made itself known. But then she glanced at the table that the three had been sitting out and she paused.

There was a cell phone sitting on the table – Slim Jim's, if she didn't miss her guess. She remembered seeing him use it when she had been interrogating him and for some reason – most likely alcohol related – he had left it behind. Even better than that, it was left on and unlocked!

Constance didn't hesitate. As quick as a whip she strode across the bar, reached out and scooped the phone up—

"What ya doing!" Eustace popped up and over her shoulder, like a snake sticking its head out of its hole. "That don't belong to you."

Eustace Burrow was a weasel of a man. And that wasn't just his personality either. His physical appearance was rodent like, from his pointed nose, to his thinning hair, to his large teeth, and right on down to the warts and boils that checkered his skin. Everything about him was rat-like and beyond unappealing.

"Never you mind," Constance said without looking back. The phone had been left unlocked, and she was quick to touch at the screen so as to keep it that way.

"I will mind!" Eustace stepped around Constance so as to plant himself in her field of view. "That don't belong to you. It belong to Slim-Jim! I know it's his cause I seen him using it." He raised his voice so as to speak over the noise of the bar. But this just made his voice come out as high and squeaky – very un-intimidating.

"Well aren't you a clever one." Constance was barely paying attention. She was scrolling through Slim-Jim's contacts, looking for Stu's number. .She wasn't at all surprised to see that it wasn't there either, adding further credence to her theory that these men were not Stu's friends.

"Give it here." Eustace snatched at the phone and Constance held it back.

"Do you mind!" she snapped, now looking at Eustace for the first time. "This is official business."

"Yeah, official Loner business," he sneered. "They my best customers and I don't want you messing it up." He snatched at the phone again, and again Constance held it out of reach.

"Your best customers?" Constance could have kicked herself for being so stupid. Of course Eustace had known them! And more than that, he had seen them the night before Stu was killed. "Eustace, can I ask you something?" For the first time – maybe ever – Constance offered Eustace a warm smile.

"Huh?" Eustace took a step back, no doubt put off by Constance's sudden change in demeanor. "You want to – what you want to ask?"

"Those three men that were sitting here. You know them?"

"I know they like to drink."

"Charming." She still held the phone, careful to not let the screen lock. "I was wondering, a few nights ago, did you happen to see if they were with a fourth man? Stu, his name is. Small guy, comb over, overbite, probably didn't look like he belonged."

"Na-ah," he shook his head. "No way."

"You're sure?" she pressed, feeling her heart beat faster by the second.

"Positive. They never drink with no-one. Or rarely anyway. What night you talking about?"

"Three nights ago," she confirmed.

"Nope. I remember too cause Slim-Jim was putting in for a speed boat on UBuyIt. He showed me it and everything! Real beauty too!" Eustace carefully reached for the phone, as if to take it from Constance without her noticing. She held it back.

"A speedboat?"

"On UBuyIt," Eustace nodded eagerly. "A real buet."

"UBuyIt?" Constance was quick on the phone, opening up an application titled 'UBuyIt.' She had no idea what the heck it was, but the first thing that came up was an image of a large speedboat with the tag 'bought' underneath it. But that wasn't what caught her eye. It was the price tag that had her gaping. The darn thing cost over one hundred thousand dollars! Her eyes nearly burst from their sockets at the sight.

"It's a good-un, huh?" Eustace nodded along as he eyed the boat. "Slim-Jim reckons when the bypass is done, he'll take me out in it too."

Constance had stopped listening. The wheels in her head were in motion as she began her search through Slim-Jim's phone, this time going through his calendar. Her first port of call was the date she knew to be Stu's birthday, and she wasn't at all surprised to see that there was no mention of it whatsoever. From there she scrolled forward in his calendar, finding numerous events planned with his two best pals, just the two.

"What you doing?" Eustace asked curiously. "I really need that phone back, Constance. If he finds out that I let you look through it, he might not let me on his boat. And if he doesn't do that, Tex-Mex might not let me take his new car for a spin."

"New car?" Constance whipped her head up to meet Eustace's searching eyes. "What new car?"

"Tex-Mex bought himself a new car – a hummer! Brand new, off the shelf." Eustace puffed his chest out importantly. "He said too that I can take it for a spin when it comes through. I love hummers, they're so big and —"

"When did he buy it?" she asked quickly.

"I dunno," Eustace shrugged. "Couple of days ago. Why?"

Constance didn't know why these purchases were so important, she just knew that they were. As a detective, one got used to finding links that others couldn't see; seeing a connection between two things that seemingly had no connection whatsoever. It was like a sixth sense. The caveat however was that even when this connection was discovered, it's meaning wasn't always clear. This was one of those times.

There was something here, something that she was missing. Tex-Mex, Slim-Jim and Piggly-Pete were clearly best friends, with no room for anyone else. They had lied to her about their friendship with Stu, and lied about what they had been arguing about the night before his death. Just like the townspeople of Modest Peak, these three were working together and if one of them was guilty, most likely they all were. Of that she was now sure. But to what end?

Furthermore, she had no doubt too that these expensive purchases were somehow involved. But again, she couldn't for the life of her figure out how they were involved. Were these three paid to kill Stu? But if so, why? Who would pay for such a thing? Again, the investigative process had turned up more questions than answers. But at least she was on the right track. Of that, Constance was sure.

"Here," Constance said absentmindedly as she handed the phone to Eustace and started for the bar's exit. Eustace eagerly took the phone back, and may have tried to say something else, but Constance wasn't listening. She was far too deep in her head for that.

In any good case both a suspect and a motive were needed. Constance had her suspects, oh she had them clear in her sights. What she was missing was the motive, the reason that they did what they had. All she need do now as find that motive, and she would have them dead to rights.

As Constance stepped from the bar and into the fading light, she caught sight of the three men, strolling down the road and into town. Now that she knew them to be guilty, the way they walked seemed to be laced with arrogance, as if they knew they had gotten away with murder. She had hated them before, but now she loathed them.

Unfortunately, there wasn't much that Constance could do about catching them. Not until she had more evidence anyway. In order to get some more, she really had two options. The first was to keep following the three and hope that something turned up. But this now seemed unlikely, and sure to be a waste of time.

The second was to turn her attention to Stu. The three men had killed him, of that she was sure. But why they had done so? Well now it was up to Constance to find out.

Chapter Twenty-One

"There's nothing here," Sheriff Nevil said with confidence as he carried the third of four large cardboard boxes into the room. "Nothing of note, anyhow."

"Are you sure about that?" Constance asked suggestively as she began to line the boxes up on the table.

"I want to say yes." Sheriff Nevil dropped the third box next to the other two. "But I also don't want to be caught with my pants down."

"We wouldn't want that."

"So, I'll say that maybe there is... and if you do find something, don't be shy about it. Heck, I'll even give you credit if you do." Despite the words spoken, the large smirk on his face suggested that he would not be giving her credit, if it came to that.

"How generous of you," Constance said dryly as she pulled the first box toward her. "Now, be a lamb will you and go get the fourth one? And then maybe make me a coffee? I feel like it's going to be a long night and if I'm going to do your job for you, I need to be awake."

Sheriff Nevil looked like he was about to argue. Most likely he was running his response over in his head, making sure that it both made sense and was scathing enough so as to let Constance know where she stood. But then he sighed, nodded his head, turned and left the room. No doubt he weighed up the pros and cons of what he was going to say, what the effect would be, and decided that in this instance it would pay to have Constance on his good side.

"Don't forget the coffee!" Constance shouted after him, chuckling to herself as she did. She was glad for the lack of argument, and even more glad that for once he was giving her his full cooperation. It was a sign as to how far the two had come when it came to working together... or how desperate he was beginning to become.

The three boxes in question – with the fourth on its way – contained all of Stu's things, as found in his bedroom at The Lone Peak. Mostly, it was a collection of clothes, books, DVD's and a few bits and bobs of little note. Where Constance should have looked through them the day she signed onto the case, Sheriff Nevil had assured her that there was nothing of interest in them. And where she had believed him at the time, now she wasn't so sure.

Really, she was desperate for a break through... or anything really. Something that gave an indication as to why he might have been murdered would have been nice. She had already been through his apartment and found nothing there, so now she was forced to look through his traveling gear; that being the things he needed to live while away on a job.

It was lucky then that Sheriff Nevil had long since resigned himself to working the case with Constance, and thus put up little to no fight when she asked to look through the boxes. She knew them to be at the station and Sheriff Nevil was only too happy to give her a room all to herself so that she could search through them. Realistically, he was probably just happy to have her out of the way. And if she did find something, well that would be beneficial too.

Unfortunately, it took Constance all of five minutes to realize that Sheriff Nevil was telling the truth when he had told her there was nothing of note in the boxes. The first three contained nothing but clothes and bathroom supplies. When Sheriff Nevil brought in the fourth – along with a coffee – her heart had skipped a beat in anticipation. But then she saw that this one was full of books and DVD's. In other words, nothing.

"Told you," he chuckled as she stuck her head into the fourth box, pulling out a book titled 'A complete and unbiased history of the state of Colorado from its conception to the present.' "Nothing."

"Don't sound so happy," she muttered as she flipped the book open, saw that it was exactly what the title claimed and then put it down.

"I'll try and contain myself." He left her alone after that, saddling from the room and closing the door behind himself.

It had been a long shot, and Constance had known it the moment she'd come across the idea. Unfortunately, she hadn't had much choice. She had her suspects clear in her sights, but she had no way of linking them to the murder. What she had been hoping was to find some sort of smoking gun, only she didn't know what the gun might look like.

Constance delved into the fourth box, pulling out more history text books, all to do with the state of Colorado. There were five of them in total and as Constance flipped through them, she found herself wondering why on earth anyone would be so darn interested in the history of the state. And that was coming from Constance, a person who prided herself on her love of home and country.

The only real piece of positive news she could glean from the experience was that it further proved that her three suspects weren't friends with Stu.

Nothing she had heard from them, or seen of Stu, suggested that they would have had anything in common. Maybe they had killed him to stop him boring them to death with talk of the state's history?

Constance was just about ready to throw in the towel. What she was going to do next, she wasn't sure of yet. But she was certain that the key to solving Stu's murder wasn't going to be found in these boxes. But then, just as she was turning to make for the door and call out to Sheriff Nevil to come and clean up after her, one of the books caught her eye.

It was a smallish book, far less conspicuous than all the others. And its title 'Colorado State: A wealth of heritage,' was as uninspired as all the others. But unlike the other books, this one was worn down beyond belief. Furthermore, there were several pages folded in on themselves, and the odd post-it sticking out too. Every other book was in excellent condition, so why was this one so busted?

Constance eyed the book for a moment, as if worried it might suddenly come to life and attack her. She then reached out and picked it up, flipping through the pages and taking note of the ones that were marked. Each one that was marked, or folded in, or posted on, was to do with sights that had significance to American Indian tribes. They were all different tribes, and were all significant for different reasons, but the link was that each to the last was heritage listed. Indeed, the word 'heritage' was circled several times.

Constance continued to flip through the book, scanning each page in search of something that would jump out. There was something here, her gut told her so. But what? And that was when she landed on the very last page.

There were two numbers scrawled on the page, both Colorado numbers, both written in the same hand writing – most likely Stu's. Constance's mouth suddenly went dry, she could feel a sense of excitement welling up inside of her. Was this something? Were these numbers important? Really, there was only one way to find out.

A quick glance toward the door, and a brief pause so as to listen if anyone was coming. With the coast clear, Constance pulled out her cell and got about dialing the first number.

Chapter Twenty-Two

"Hello?" The voice on the other end of the line was soft and quietly spoken, sounding like it belonged to an elderly gentleman. Most importantly, Constance didn't recognize it.

"Hello," Constance started. "May I ask who it is that I am speaking to."

There was a brief pause. "You want to know who – you called me." The man on the other end of the line didn't sound angry at least, or put out. Just appropriately surprised.

"I know and I'm sorry. But I really do need to know to whom I'm speaking." Constance did her best to sound polite, and even genial. She needed whoever this was to know she wasn't a threat, and thus divulge as much information as possible. That was assuming he had any information to give.

"Can I inquire first to whom I am speaking," the man pressed.

Constance sighed, quickly realizing that whoever this was wasn't about to lay himself bare for any old random caller to see. "My name is Constance Aberfield and I live in Modest Peak. I was calling to —"

"Oh, Modest Peak!" The man exclaimed merrily on the other end of the line. "Founded in 1709, not officially recognized until fifty years after the fact, it was the mountain range that drew the first settlers. They believed, or rather hoped, that they could mine the range, possibly for gold or silver. Of course, they knew little about such things and came up empty handed. But from what I understand, the town still thrives, relying on highway traffic for the majority of its economic growth."

"That's... that's right." Constance had been standing, and was forced to take a seat as this man, whoever he was, rattled off information about her town that even Constance didn't know. It was as if he had a text book right in front of him and was reading from it.

"I should hope so," he chortled. "I wrote the book on the place."

"You... I'm sorry, who are you?" Constance had a pretty good feeling that this time, he was going to tell her.

"Oh, how rude. My name is Gerald Huff, author and historian. No doubt you've heard of me. Well, you called me, so I would say that odds are pretty high. Always good to speak to a fan." He was beamed, or at least it sounded as if he were.

The name definitely rang a bell and Constance knew why. As he spoke, her eyes moved down to the table, to the book from which she had gotten this number. On the front cover, underneath the title, was the author's name, one Gerald Huff. She had called the book's author!

"I am such a fan," she lied effortlessly, sensing it would do her good. "Sorry about before, I just had to be sure that I was speaking to the right person."

"Don't worry yourself," he dismissed happily. "Like I said, I'm always happy to speak to a fan. And you said you're from Modest Peak?"

"Indeed. I'm so glad you've heard of it – and then some!"

"Of course I have! Although I confess, that little spiel I gave you a moment ago wasn't completely from memory. I was reading up on the town just a few days ago. Funny how things work, isn't it?"

"You were?" she asked surprised. "Can I ask why – I mean, not that I blame you. But Modest Peak, of all places? Odd that you'd be reading up on my little mountain town." Constance hurried to the door of the room and popped her head out, just to double check that no one was coming. She was on to something, she could feel it, and didn't want to be disturbed.

"Your town has become a recent subject in a paper I'm publishing, or rather one that I'm thinking of publishing. Truth be told I would have missed it entirely were it not for a keen fan of mine giving me a call and bringing it to my attention. Isn't it funny how the world works!"

"The paper you're publishing. Can I ask what it's for?"

"Another fan!" Gerald could not have sounded more pleased. Something told Constance that he didn't get too many random calls and was relishing in it. "The paper doesn't have a title yet, but I've been tracking the movements of a lost American Indian Tribe called the Nowraese and if my research is correct, they made camp right by Modest Peak some two-hundred and fifty years ago."

"Made camp?"

"Lived, for some time," he corrected. "Another fan of mine – although I guess he's more of a fellow researcher at this point, all the work he's put in, stumbled upon the site and called me personally. I'm yet to make it out and look for myself, but from what he's told me, well it's almost fact at this point. Isn't that just wonderful."

"It is," she said quickly, mind racing. "And this researcher? Can I ask his name – I mean, I most likely know him and would just die to have a chat."

"Most certainly. Remind me to get his number for you too, and his email. His name is Stu Starky, a construction worker of some sort he tells me, but with a keen interest in the historical and the geometrical. We've never met, but that will be amended. Oh, how I love meeting fans!"

Constance was struck speechless. If she hadn't already been sitting down, she might have just fallen over. Indeed, she nearly dropped the cell phone before regaining just enough of herself to hang on to it for dear life as she slunk into her seat and let what she had just heard wash over her.

"Hello? Hello? Ms. Aberfield?" Gerald called down the line, sounding a little worried. "Are you there?"

"What – oh, yes. Sorry," she quickly apologized. All she had just learned was still being processed, so Constance decided to press for more information as a means to speed it up. "I'm sorry to pester you, but can I clarify something?"

"My dear, I love being pestered."

"Excellent." She sat up straight, gathered her thoughts and pressed on. "So, you're publishing a paper on the movements of a lost tribe known as the Nowarise —"

"Nowraese," he corrected.

"And was this paper known to anyone else – I mean, did anyone know that you were working on it?"

"Just those in the circle. Fellow buffs and such."

"And Stu Starky, he called you a few days ago. Maybe a week, to let you know that he may have found a site that this tribe had settled on some time ago?"

"You can imagine my shock! I've been tracking this tribe for the better part of five years. But gosh darn there was a huge portion of their journey missing. And I mean fifty years or so worth. And then out of the blue, Stu calls me, claiming he found the missing piece. I tell you Ms. Aberfield, I nearly fell over in my chair I was so surprised."

"And it's in Modest Peak?" she confirmed. The pieces were all coming together. She just needed a little more.

"About ten miles out," he corrected. "Like I said, I haven't seen the site yet – oh that's reminds me! You don't happen to know if the construction has been halted, do you? I've been meaning to get out there as quick as I can, but funds are a little tight."

"Construction? Halted?" Her mouth was as dry as any desert in the world. She licked her lips, but to no avail.

"The bypass," he continued. "That's how Stu found the site. Apparently, a bypass is being built right through the middle of the site. Stu assured me he was going to do all he could to stop it until I made it out to have a look. Do you know if he succeeded? I haven't had a chance to call him yet."

"And if what Stu said is right? That what he found is the site of this tribe, the Nowraese? What would that mean for the bypass? Or the area in general?" Constance's heart rate was up. She just needed a little more...

"Why, I would imagine that the site would become heritage listed. It would if I had anything to say, and believe me, I usually have a lot to say."

"So, the bypass would stop indefinitely?"

"Without a doubt." He paused, as if letting the information sink in. "Has it been paused, do you know? Like I said, I'm yet to call Stu back."

This was it. This was what Constance had been looking for. The link! Stu had found out about the site, had spoken to this Gerald character, and then gone about trying to stop the bypass from being built until Gerald was able to come out and see for himself. Heck, he was trying to stop the bypass entirely.

Constance thought back to the night before Stu had died, that argument she had overheard. Was it possible that was what the men had been fighting about? The reason they were so mad with Stu? But then again, why? Why would those three care so much about a silly bypass? Surely, they weren't being paid enough to be that effected by it. Unless —

"Hello? Hello? Ms. Aberfield?" Gerald called down the line again. "Are you there?"

"Sorry," she shook her head. "I am. I got a little lost in my thoughts."

"That's fine," he said merrily. "I was just saying, I know that Stu was going to call the head honcho and see about stopping the bypass before it ruined what could be valuable land. You don't know if he managed to, do you?"

"The head honcho?" Constance racked her brain to try and think of who this might be.

"Brumbry, I believe his name was. Mayor Brumbry."

Again, Constance felt the need to sit, even though she already was. It felt like she had been punched in the stomach. Like someone had swiped the legs out from underneath her. Like she had just sprinted a mile and now needed a moment to cool down, lest she overheat and die! It was all too much.

Stu, a fan of this Gerald, had found links to a paper that the historian was working on. Even better was that this link just happened to sit smack dab in the middle of where the new bypass was going to go. He had gone out of his way to call Gerald, let him know what he had found, and then promise he would hold off the bypass until Gerald himself could confirm. And then, just to add a cherry to the top of what was already a delicious cake, if Gerald was able to confirm all of this, the bypass might have been canceled entirely.

Constance had been pulling her hair out to find a motive of some kind, to find some reason that someone, anyone, would want Stu dead. Well she had just found one. The only problem, if it could be called that, was that her initial suspects appeared innocent. She would have loved to have tried and lay the blame at Tex-Mex, Slim-Jim and Piggly-Pete's feet, but that now seemed unlikely. Mayor Brumbry was at fault here, at least as far as she saw it.

The conversation with Gerald didn't go for too much longer, mainly just because Constance didn't want to tell him that Stu was dead, and she also didn't want to lie to him either. So, she thanked him for his help, promised that Stu would call as soon as he was able, and then she hung up. By the time she was done, she was covered in a thin gleam of sweat and puffing and panting.

Now that she had a moment to think, she got about putting the evidence together, hoping it would make more sense. And it did... to a fashion. She was now certain that the mayor had killed Stu so as to keep the heritage site under wraps. She also had her sneaking suspicions that the other three may have helped in some way, possibly hiding the body for a large fee. That would explain those expensive purchases too! She felt giddy over the chance to tie them to this somehow.

Yes, it all fit snugly. Like a glove. She had her man, and possibly men. Now all she had to was prove it.

It was just then, as all of this new information started to sit comfortably on her shoulders, that Constance looked back down at the book and remembered that there was another number scribbled under the first. Absolutely bursting at the seams with curiosity, Constance called the number.

"Hello?" the very recognizable voice of Mayor Brumbry answered on the other end of the line. Constance hung the phone up immediately.

Not that it was needed, but that call was the final nail in the coffin. Stu had at one point called the mayor, most likely telling him what he had found out, and in doing so had signed his own death warrant.

Finally, Constance had her man. Now all she needed to do was prove it.

***

"You need me to do what?" Sheriff Nevil asked incredulously, only half paying attention as he eyed the plate of food sitting in front of him.

"I haven't gotten that far yet," she snapped before she could help herself. "I mean..." she took a deep breath as a means to calm down. "... You know that I haven't explained that yet. Just listen, will you?"

Sheriff Nevil was seated on his couch at home, and from the looks of things, was just about to tuck into a home cooked meal before Constance nearly knocked his door down and barged into his house. Now his meal was getting cold as Constance stormed back and forth across his living room, throwing her hands in the air as she tried to explain her plan to him, all the while hoping that he would go along. And it was quite the plan too.

"Explain it all to me again – I was distracted." He held his hands up in defense as if sensing that Constance was about to explode. "The smell of my baked potato and roasted lamb had me salivating. Sorry if I was only half paying attention."

Constance would have loved to have snapped at him, given him an ear full, or better yet, throw his meal across the room as a means to make a point. But she also sensed that wouldn't have done much good, especially considering that she needed his help, and that this help required him committing some suspect acts that weren't exactly worthy of his position as Sheriff.

So, she didn't snap. Instead, she sat down opposite him, made sure that she had his full attention and then got about explaining what she had come over here to explain. It had taken her the better part of the afternoon to put it all together and now that it was, she needed him to hear it all... and then agree how wonderful she was at having come up with it.

And so, Constance started her story where all good stories started, at the beginning, with Mayor Brumbry.

"The bypass is his last shot at getting elected," she explained to Sheriff Nevil. "Without it, he doesn't have a chance. Trust me, I spoke to his receptionist – heck, I saw his office. He's hung his entire campaign on this thing and if it isn't done by the time the elections role around in a few months, he'll be looking for a new job. So, in other words, he's desperate."

Sheriff Nevil frowned and nodded as he dug into his dinner. Long, slow bites before swallowing, as if he was really savoring each mouthful. But Constance knew him well enough to know he was paying attention, and so she continued.

"And that's where Stu comes in. He's a surveyor for the site and during one of his... I don't know what they're called. While he was out in the field, he must have come across the site that he believes to be linked to this Nowraese tribe. Honestly, the luck that he found it at all. I'd say that he and maybe five other people, if that, even knew of its existence. So naturally he was excited."

"And that's when he called this Professor Gerald?" Sheriff Nevil asked thickly, through a mouthful of lamb.

"I don't know the exact timeline, but I would say so," Constance confirmed, glad that he was following along. "I would predict that he called Gerald to tell him what he found and Gerald asked if Stu would be able to stall the bypass until he could come down and see it for himself."

Sheriff Nevil swallowed his mouthful, nodding along the whole while. "And then what?"

"Well, the next is all guess work. But I think you'll agree that it makes perfect sense. Kind of a 'fill in the blanks,' but with an ending." Constance nodded her assurance to Sheriff Nevil, as if willing him into believing her. He frowned at her, letting her know that he wasn't going to be led to a conclusion so simply. She'd have to earn it.

Really, there was no need for her to worry, as the facts pretty much spoke for themselves. From what she gathered, based off all she had learned, Stu went to either Mayor Brumbry or Foreman Joe with the information learned, most likely telling them of the sites importance and then asking for a halt in the bypass until the correct measures could be taken. No doubt this information wasn't well received, which led Stu to making his next big mistake.

"Which was?" Sheriff Nevil inquired as he took a sip of his beer, something that he always had with dinner.

"I don't know," she admitted. But then she quickly added, "But I would guess that it involved him not dropping the case. Maybe he made some calls, or threatened too? Whatever he did, it got Mayor Brumbry anxious enough that he went to Tex-Mex, Slim-Jim and Piggly-Pete to take care of the problem."

"Tex-what?" Sheriff Nevil asked.

"Those three workers I was telling you about. I'll bet you anything that Mayor Brumbry bribed them to either kill Stu, or hide the body once he was done. I know for a fact that the three are spending beyond their means, which means that they must have been given a bundle. Stu is dead, and all of them have their fingers in it."

And that was that. Constance dusted off her hands and got to her feet as if indicating that she had finished, wrapped up, and was good to go. But really, she was only just getting started.

"Where are you going?" Sheriff Nevil asked without moving.

"Nowhere," she responded sheepishly. "I just... never mind." She took her seat again, settled herself down, and then started back up. "So, what do you think?"

There was a pause. A long one. One that had Sheriff Nevil chewing his food so darn slowly that Constance was sure it would go cold in his mouth. And even once he finished chewing, and swallowing, he took a long, deep sip of his drink until —

"Come on!"

"All right," he eased. "I was just thinking. Look, I'm not an idiot, and we've been through this all enough times now that I know when to listen. You're rarely wrong in this, and the few times I've thought you were, it's come back to bite me."

"Rog, that might be the nicest thing you have ever said."

"Don't get used to it." He smirked for a moment, before continuing. "With that being said, it's a good theory and the odds are that it's probably true. But you know as well as I do that the job is only half done. We need to prove it. So, unless you have any of that proof lying around, I ask again. What now?"

Now it was Constance's turn to smirk. She did just that, leaning back in her chair with her arms folded over her chest. She had a plan, it was a good one, and she could not wait to see what Sheriff Nevil thought.

"Rog," she started smugly. "I thought you were never going to ask."

Chapter Twenty-Three

The plan had a lot of moving pieces, with each one needing to work in perfect sync if Constance and Sheriff Nevil had any chances of catching their man... or men, as Constance predicated it would be.

The first port of call, was going to be none other than seeing Eustace at The Loner. Constance hated that they had to ask him for help, but she hated failing even more than that, so she figured she could look past it this one time. She and Sheriff Nevil found Eustace exactly where they thought they would, in his bar.

"You want me to give them free drinks all day?" Eustace asked incredulously. "For free?" he then confirmed. He was standing behind the bar, polishing the same glass he had been since Constance and Sheriff Nevil walked inside. Despite this consistent polish, the glass was as dirty as ever.

"Not for free," Constance sighed. They'd explained this already to him, but he was choosing to be purposefully dense. "Just tell them it's free. We will both happily cover all costs later in the day."

"How can I trust ya?" he sneered and narrowed his eyes.

Sheriff Nevil seemed to take personal offense at this, standing himself up and leaning over Eustace so as to assert his authority. "Are you honestly questioning the integrity of the Sheriff of Modest Peak?" he warned.

"No, no," Eustace cowered. "Just double checking is all. Can't be too careful."

"Look." Constance sighed again and rubbed at her eyes. "I'm about to send the three in here, all right. Your job is just to keep them here for as long as you can." She and Sheriff Nevil also had a lie they had conceived for why the drinks would be free. They quickly explained it to Eustace.

"And if they want to leave?" he asked.

"Free drinks?" she scoffed. "Yeah, I can't see them going anywhere."

Eustace was naturally difficult, but eventually he came around. Really, the idea of pouring free drinks all day, knowing that they would eventually be paid back, was probably too much to resist. Men drank more when they thought it free and no doubt Eustace was already seeing dollar signs.

The next part of the plan was probably the easiest to pull off, and Constance got about doing it the moment they left Eustace's bar. A quick right turn saw her back in her hotel, and a few hurried steps up the staircase put her outside of Tex-Mex's bedroom. She knocked three times.

"Come in!" he shouted from within the room.

Constance popped her head in, holding her breath just in case the room stunk... which it most likely would. Tex-Mex lay on his bed, bathing in the mid-morning sun that streamed through the window. With no work to do for the day, he had evidently resigned himself to a day of leisure.

"What do you want?" he asked without so much as glancing at Constance.

"I'm doing a favor for a friend," Constance started casually. "Eustace from next door, you know him?"

"I do." Tex-Mex sat up slightly, his interest increasing.

"I just spoke to him and he told me something about his beer supply going stale in a day's time? Apparently, he can't get rid of it. I'm no barkeep so I don't know the specifics —"

"So?" he cut in.

"Well, Eustace asked that I let you know that beer will be free all day. Or at least until the tap runs out —"

Tex-Mex couldn't be up and out of his bed fast enough. A second later and his was shuffling into a shirt and shoes and one more after that and he was on his way toward the door, just about throwing Constance from her feet in a bid to get past. She stood in the doorway once he was gone, watching as Tex-Mex hurried to collect his two friends. It was almost too easy sometimes.

The third step to the plan involved Foreman Joe. Constance and Sheriff Nevil had both pondered long and hard about Foreman Joe, trying to decide if he was involved in some way. In the end, they both agreed that he was not. Not only was he appropriately put out over the disappearance of Stu on the morning of his death, but Sheriff Nevil pulled some strings and got a sneak peek at his paycheck. It was a lot of money... a lot of money. Constance doubted that he could be convinced to commit murder for a little more.

Even with Foreman Joe not involved in the murder, they still needed him out of the way. He was a key part of the plan after all. It was because of this that Sheriff Nevil put in a personal call to Foreman Joe, asking him to meet them at the station immediately.

Foreman Joe arrived at the station about fifteen minutes after Constance had informed Tex-Mex of the free booze. He strode into the station, looking appropriately annoyed at having to come down. He didn't know why he had to come down either, and Constance knew that when he found out he would be even more furious.

"You're kidding?" he growled as Sheriff Nevil explained why he had been called. The two sat in one of the interrogation rooms, a stack of cardboard boxes between them.

"I wish I was." Sheriff Nevil held his hands up in defense. "But that's the bureaucracy for you. Honestly, if you start now and go quick, it shouldn't take you any more than an hour or so."

"And what if I do a half-job? Which I will," he warned through gritted teeth.

"I expect you too," Sheriff Nevil chuckled as he rose from his seat and pushed the chair in. "No one checks this stuff anyhow – expect the lawyers. But it probably won't get that far. And sorry." Sheriff Nevil offered a sympathetic smile before turning and leaving the room... and Foreman Joe in it, alone.

Constance watched the performance from the comfort of the adjoining room, through the two-way mirror. Although she didn't hate Foreman Joe or anything like that, she also wasn't a huge fan of his either. It felt nice, using him this way and she chose to see it as a form of payback for the way he had treated her in the past.

"I give it an hour," Sheriff Nevil warned as he strode into the room. "After that, he'll probably be so fed up he'll go and commit murder himself."

"That's fine," Constance said. "An hour is all we need."

They had to keep Foreman Joe out of the way. That was it. He needed to be unreachable for roughly an hour, and that was when Constance came up with the idea to keep him at the station until it was all done with. In order to keep him there, Sheriff Nevil called him in and claimed that he needed to go through all the interrogation transcripts for each worker that had been interviewed after Stu's murder. He had to read and then verify that each sounded accurate, as he was the only person that knew each worker personally. There were over fifty of them in all, and each went for several minutes. It was no wonder he was mad.

But again, the lie was conceived to keep him out of the way, and now that it was done, they could get on to the next part of the plan, the final part, that part that would make or break the case. Mayor Brumbry was the final piece of this puzzle and they found him exactly where they thought they would, at the site, trying to find a way to get things moving again.

As Sheriff Nevil pulled his police car onto the site, Constance watched the mayor with curiosity. He wasn't doing anything of interest, which was why Constance was so fascinated. He was kind of just pacing the site, looking at pieces of equipment and throwing his hands in the air in frustration. Constance guessed that he was just angry about the site still being closed down, and felt that his being there in person might have some sort of positive effect. But she also chose to see it as a good thing. The man was desperate, and that would be needed.

The sight of Sheriff Nevil's car coming to a stop had the expected effect on the mayor. He raced for the car, a kick to his step, wringing his hands together and licking his lips in anticipation. Even before Sheriff Nevil was out of the car, the mayor had him bailed up.

"Sheriff!" Mayor Brumbry called as he hurried toward the car. "Give me some good news!"

"Mayor Brumbry," Sheriff Nevil started warily as he closed the door behind him. The idea was to appear forlorn, even upset. Constance eyed him as she too climbed from the car and walked to meet him, smirking to herself over his performance. "I was hoping to find you here."

"Yes, yes," the mayor dismissed. "I figured I may as well be here, in case something new came up – did it? Tell me something good. Please!"

"It's not good," Sheriff Nevil bowed his head. "Foreman Joe has ordered that the site remain closed until —"

"What?!" Mayor Brumbry exclaimed. "When? Why?!"

Sheriff Nevil grimaced, as if put out by the interruption. "He sought me out earlier to ask how the investigation was coming along. I told him that it had slowed to a crawl. He asked what that meant for the bypass and —"

"What did you tell him?" Mayor Brumbry cut in. He was clenching his fists with such force that Constance worried he might draw blood.

"I told him the choice lay with him. This case is going to take longer than I thought, and I know that I can't keep the site closed forever. So, I said to him that if he feels confident reopening and getting back to work, so be it. I can't stop him."

Mayor Brumbry let go a huge sigh of relief, looking like a weight had just been lifted from his shoulders. "Thank God," he exhaled. "That's... wait."

Then it dawned on him. "You said that he wanted to keep the site closed? — that's what you just said!"

"That's what I came here to tell you. Joe is sick to death of all the stopping and starting. He said he'd rather wait until the case was solved and he could work without all the interruptions. Regardless of how long it took."

"He said that?" Mayor Brumbry's face darkened.

"He did. Then I said, what if someone else was hired? A new foreman? I know how bad you want this job done."

"And?" Mayor Brumbry pushed, face eager.

"He said, no." Sheriff Nevil crossed his arms and exhaled as if confused. "I guess he wants to finish what he started? I don't know. But I figured I should be the one to tell you, what, with him being gone and all."

"Gone where?"

"Back to Denver for the day. He'll be back tomorrow, so I guess you can speak to him then. Try and make him change his mind. Honestly, it's up to you what you do."

"I see..." Mayor Brumbry had stopped paying attention. Constance had to hide her satisfied smirk as she watched him retreat into his own head, no doubt already concocting his next move. "So, if Foreman Joe quit, then...?"

"That's on you," Sheriff Nevil shrugged. "Like I said, I'm just the messenger. If it was me, I'd try and talk him around. But you've met the man."

"He's a wall," Mayor Brumbry nodded his agreement.

There was a moment after that in which nothing was said. Mayor Brumbry was long gone, staring into the distance, lost in his own thoughts. Sheriff Nevil and Constance said nothing too, waiting for the mayor to break the silence. They needed him to come to his own conclusion, and then hopefully try and follow it through.

"Mayor Brumbry?" Constance eventually pressed after some time.

"What – oh, yes." He jumped on the spot and shook his head to himself. "I'm sorry I've... I've got to go." And he did. Without another word, he turned and scurried away and toward his car.

Constance and Sheriff Nevil watched him go. Constance was beaming to herself, Sheriff Nevil looked uncertain. "You think it will work?" he asked.

"There's only one way to tell." She checked the time, seeing that it had been about thirty minutes since her visit to Tex-Mex's room. "I think we better be going."

And that was that. The plan was in motion and now all there was to do was wait and see if it worked. Constance, in her usual cocky manner, wasn't in the least concerned. She knew her plan would work, it was just a matter of being there when it did.

***

Constance and Sheriff Nevil sat crouched by the back-door entrance into The Loner. What it was, was a kind of foyer area, separating the bar itself from the alley that the bar backed on to. It was such a small space that it barely fit the one person, let alone two. And yet, both Constance and the sheriff crouched down together, dealing with the uncomfortable circumstance for the sake of the case.

190

"How long has it been?" groaned Sheriff Nevil as he rubbed at his thighs.

"One minute longer than the last time you asked," Constance snapped. "Now, be quiet. I can barely hear as it is."

The door into the bar was cracked open just a touch, enough so that Constance could peer through and see the nearest table to the door, one that just happened to seat Tex-Mex, Piggly-Pete and Slim-Jim. It was the same table they had sat at the other day when she had followed them, and she had guessed – correctly – that it was their favorite.

The bar was rather empty, which was more on account of luck than anything else. But this allowed for the conversation of the three men to carry through the bar and into the back-foyer, so that Constance and Sheriff Nevil could listen to all that was said... well, sort of. They had to really listen, and a lot of what was said was lost in translation. But they got the gist, and that would be enough.

"God they talk some junk, don't they?" Sheriff Nevil grumbled.

"Will you be quiet," she snapped again.

He was right, though. From what she had heard so far, the majority of their conversation revolved around women, drinking and drugs. There was a lot of laughter too, although not at anything particularly funny, and even more personal insults. And that wasn't to mention the bodily secretions! Honestly, the world would be a better place with these men behind bars... which they would be, very soon. At least if Constance had her way.

They had been crouching in that foyer for the better part of twenty minutes, ever since they arrived back from speaking to the mayor. And it was after those long, uncomfortable twenty minutes, that Constance started to seriously doubt herself and her plan. In fact, she was all but ready to admit defeat... and then she saw the front door swing open.

"He's here!" she gasped excitedly. "He's here!"

It was Mayor Brumbry. He threw the front door to the bar open, spotted the three men sitting and drinking at the back of the bar, and just about ran to meet them.

"There you are!" he exclaimed, not even bothering to keep his voice down. "I've been looking everywhere for you. Don't you answer your phones?!"

"Everywhere?" Tex-Mex chuckled. "You'd think the bar would be the first place. More!" Tex-Mex turned and indicated to Eustace for another round of drinks.

"It's 11am," the mayor pointed out as he took a seat with the three men. "Excuse me if I didn't think to check."

"You're excused," Slim-Jim chuckled as he finished off his beer. It was just then that Eustace popped up by the table with three more glasses of beer. The three men grabbed at them eagerly, giving their thanks to Eustace as they did.

"I need to speak to you." Mayor Brumbry leaned across the table, dropping his voice to a whisper so that Constance had to open the door a tad more so as to hear.

"About?" Tex-Mex asked as he chugged on his ale.

"I've got another job." Constance's heart skipped a beat as the mayor spoke those words. She was right! She knew she was right!

"Job?" Piggly-Pete asked stupidly. "The bypass?"

"No, not the bypass!" Mayor Brumbry snapped. He then realized he was shouting and again dropped his voice. "One like the last time... with Stu..."

"You want us to kill Stu?" Slim-Jim piped up. "We already did that."

"Will you keep it down!" Mayor Brumbry gasped. He looked around the bar, double checking that no one was listening. Only when he was satisfied, did he continue. "Not Stu. Someone else... obviously!"

"The price?" Tex-Mex asked, almost sounding bored as he did.

"Same as last time," the mayor confirmed. "Half before, and half when it's done."

"And the target?" Tex-Mex confirmed in the same nonchalant manner.

"Foreman Joe." This got the appropriate reaction. Piggly-Pete spat up his drink. Slim-Jim's eyes popped open in surprise. Tex-Mex, although still appearing bored, couldn't help but look slightly shocked. "Is that okay?" Mayor Brumbry pressed.

"Why you want him dead?" Slim-Jim asked.

"It doesn't matter."

"It does," Tex-Mex backed up. "He's our boss. Tied to us directly. He goes missing, you don't think people will come see us?"

"I just need him out of the way – and hidden!" Mayor Brumbry growled. "Not just dumped somewhere that anyone can find him."

"We didn't just dump the last one," Slim-Jim warned. "We buried him good. Not our fault that old bat from the hotel went digging."

"Yeah!" Piggly-Pete pipped up. "We buried him deep."

"It doesn't matter," Mayor Brumbry eased, keeping his voice low. "A yes or no. That's all I need. Will you do it – today, if you can?"

There was a pause as the three men looked to one another. Really, it was two of the men looking to Tex-Mex for an answer, as he was the group's leader. There was a lot of eyebrow raising, held tilting and shrugging until, "Fine," Tex-Mex agreed. "We'll do it."

"Thank you," Mayor Brumbry sighed. He then pushed himself to his feet. "You know how to reach me."

"You going?" Tex-Mex asked. "We got free drinks here!"

"Yes, I'm going. I can't afford to be seen with you. Even for a second would be detrimental."

Constance had been so lost in the moment that she hadn't even noticed Sheriff Nevil stand up behind her, step over her shoulders and stride into the bar; not until he was well and truly inside the establishment anyway. The sight of him had her jumping from her skin, worried that he was going to ruin everything. But then she realized that the sting operation had worked, and he was just doing what needed to be done.

"Too late for that," Sheriff Nevil said coolly as she strode into the bar and right up to the mayor. "I see you."

Mayor Brumbry could not have looked more shocked. Eyes like dinner plates, he glanced at the entrance, as if trying to decide if it were worth running or not. "Sheriff!" he exclaimed a little too loudly. "What a pleasant —"

"Save it," Sheriff Nevil warned. "I heard it all, loud and clear as day. You, Mayor Brumbry, have been rather busy."

"I... I... they... it's not... we..."

"Well... dang." Tex-Mex didn't make to run. He barely even moved. Instead he remained seated, sipping on his beer like he had all the time in the world. "Didn't see that coming."

And that was that. Constance walked into the bar next, a huge smile on her face, one that she shared with the three men. She looked to each, meeting their eyes, making sure that they knew she was the one that had caught them. Tex-Mex looked unimpressed. Slim-Jim looked like he was about to cry and Piggly-Pete looked confused, like he hadn't quite worked out what was going on.

And as for Mayor Brumbry? Constance had seen men cry before, but nothing like this. On his knees, hands held together as if in prayer, he wept and blubbered as Sheriff Nevil put on the handcuffs and read him his rights. It was a sad display to say the least, but it was no less than what he deserved.

"Eustace!" Constance called out to the barkeep, currently cowering behind the bar. "Another round, I think. On me. It's going to be the last one these gents have for a while."

Chapter Twenty-Four

"Done and done." Jonas stood behind Constance, dusting his hands together, as if congratulating himself on a job well done. Personally, Constance didn't see what all the fuss was about, he had barely done anything.

"Not quite," she reminded him as she pointed to the computer screen in front of the two. She was sitting in her office chair, counting the seconds until she could stand. "I still have to send it live."

"Go live," Jonas chuckled. He leaned back over her shoulder, his right hand going for the mouse. "And I figured that I'd let you do the honors?"

"How chivalrous of you."

"It's more self-preservation. If you wake up in the middle of the night and change your mind, you'll only have yourself to blame." He gave her shoulder a playful squeeze with his left hand.

"Surely, you don't think I'm that petty?" She rested her hand on his, returning the squeeze.

"Do you want me to answer that?" he joked.

"Careful," she warned. She then took his hand and gave the back of it a kiss. "Come on, we may as well get it over and done with." She took the mouse from Jonas, guided the cursor over the screen and then clicked a little button that read 'upload.' "There," she said with a forced, satisfied smile. "Live."

The two were working on The Lone Peak's website, and had been for the better part of the day. Where Constance was sure that all she needed to do was select a font and be done with it, little problems kept on popping up and delaying their finish. It was just lucky that she had Jonas with her, otherwise she would have given up a long time ago... after throwing the computer across the room.

"It looks good," Jonas noted as he wrested the mouse off her and scrolled through the freshly launched site. "Now we wait for the bookings to come rolling in. I predict a frenzy."

"Ha, ha."

Truth be told, Constance had very nearly decided against launching the site. Oh sure, she, Jonas and Dakota had put many, many hours into building it. And yes, it would inevitably be a good thing as far as the business went. But as far as she saw things, it just wasn't necessary. At least not anymore.

The bypass was no longer an issue. After the arrest was made of Mayor Brumbry, Tex-Mex, Slim-Jim and Piggly-Pete, it was put on hold until further notice. Before this notice could be reached, Gerald the historian flew into town, took a look at the site for himself and confirmed that yes, it was once used as a camping ground by the Nowraese tribe. This was enough to have the entire area heritage listed, which meant that the bypass was canceled indefinitely. Modest Peak was saved.

The entire town celebrated this fact, even those that were forced to pay very hefty fines on account of their interference with the case. Despite these fines, Mr. Trunch, Mr. Buck and the brother and sister duo of Dakota and Dexter could not have been happier. As far as they were concerned, it was thanks to them that the bypass was canceled, and if they had to pay some fines, well those were the breaks.

Of all the businesses in town that benefited the most from the bypass being canceled, The Lone Peak

Hotel was undoubtedly at the top of the list. It relied primarily on highway traffic for business, and Constance was sure that no number of websites could trump this fact.

"Hey, I'm proud of you," Jonas continued, his hand still resting on her shoulder. This time he leaned forward and planted a kiss on top of her head too. "Seriously."

"What for?" Constance frowned. "Solving the murder? That was a week ago!"

"No, not that," he laughed. "For going through with this website. You could have not bothered. In fact, I half expected you to."

Constance purposefully exhaled as she pushed her seat out and stood. "Jonas, it's as if you don't even know me," she joked. She turned on her heel and wrapped her arms around her husband's waist.

"I know you pretty well," he smirked as he wrapped his arms around her also, pulling her in nice and close.

"Then you know how much I love change," she pointed out. "In fact, I'm pretty sure I was the one that suggested the website."

For a moment, Jonas clearly thought she was being serious. He opened his mouth to protest, only to see the smirk on her lips and the smile behind her eyes. Joining in on the smile, he shook his head. "You're right. What was I thinking?" he laughed.

"Come on." Letting go of Jonas, Constance stepped around her husband and made for the door. "Eleanor should be arriving pretty soon. Won't it be nice to be out on the road and greet her when she pulls up? Oh how I've missed her."

"I didn't know you were looking that forward to her coming back?" Jonas took her hand and led her through the door. "I thought you liked change?"

"Hey," she warned. "I may like change, but some things are best left alone. That includes good friends. And as much as I liked Dakota... well, I never thought that I'd miss Eleanor and Sydney working here. Yet here we are."

Jonas laughed at this, shaking his head at the thought. Two worse workers didn't exist, but as Constance pointed out, some things were best left as they were. And so, together, Constance and Jonas made for the curb out front of the hotel, eager to greet Eleanor as she returned from her holiday. Soon after that, Sydney would be coming back too and then, finally, everything would be back to the way it was.